Found Christmas

by

Jeanette Collins

Found Christmas

Cover Art by *Debbie Taylor*

The Wild Rose Press, Inc.
PO Box 708
Adams Basin, NY 14410-0708
Visit us at www.thewildrosepress.com

Publishing History
First Edition, 2021
Trade Paperback ISBN 978-1-5092-3574-2
Digital ISBN 978-1-5092-3575-9

Published in the United States of America

Finding the staircase too narrow for three, Letty went ahead. Bia took his weight as she was able. They haltingly made it up, step by step, his arm close around her. She smelled his hair and skin, perspiration, and horseflesh. A tremor passed over her spine, an awareness. When she glanced up at his face, he looked down at her, his blue eyes questioning.

They reached the landing as Letty ran ahead to the third chamber and lit the lamps. Bia got him down the hall to the spare room and the bed. Letty turned back the cover. He sat down, breathing hard, the blanket around him. Bia gazed at his knees, fuzzy blond calves, and remarkable feet.

"That was a trek. I do thank you, ladies. I am ever in your debt."

"We will leave you to be comfortable. Another blanket is there. If you require anything, call out. I hope you can rest."

Bia left the room and, in the hall, waited. Letty quietly asked, "So what was it? Some awful Frenchman cut your side?"

She flattened to the wall, listening.

"A soldier just tried to save himself. Go along, Miss Letty. I am a tired man."

"Never mind. Rest. We will talk later."

"My hearty thanks. And to you, too, Miss Bianca," he called.

Bia blushed hotly as Letty sauntered from the room and closed the door. "Is he not splendid, Bia?" she whispered excitedly.

She propelled her sister back to the stairs. "He can fill whole pages. But tomorrow, he will be gone. We had no lunch. It must be time for tea, do you not think?"

Chapter One

Kent, England, Tuesday, December 1815

Bianca Greenway woke as the bed sagged. She opened one eye, and Woof licked her chin.

"Wake up, Bia, wake up!" her sister cried. "It snowed!"

She moved the dog aside. "Did it?"

"Yes, lots." Letty pulled at the covers. "Put on clothes and let us go out."

Bia yawned. "After breakfast."

"No, no, that will not do. It might melt, then we shall have no Christmas at all. We must go out and cut holly branches."

Bia petted the shepherd's shaggy ears. "Is there holly hereabouts?"

"We have to look for it. That is the way it is supposed to happen. It snows, then everyone in the house party goes out. A merry time is had, with mistletoe and the like."

"What book is this?"

"Mine! The one I am writing." Letty tugged the comforter away. "Come now. Just for an hour, then we can breakfast."

Woof wagged his tail, his doggy expression hopeful.

"Very well."

Her sister leapt off the bed, Woof right after her, and ran out the door.

Bia got up and, in her nightie, searched through the armoire. In a bottom drawer, she found old trousers and jerseys. She held up the old-fashioned pantaloons. They would fit, or nearly, and she would not spoil her clothing. She took a pair and went next door to Letty's room.

"Look here, Letty. Wear these and save your gowns."

Letty stared. "Pantaloons?"

"Old style, but they are wool. Give them a try. And there are a few jerseys. Come back when you are ready."

Bia put on stockings and the dark plaid pantaloons. They reached her ankles, so would do nicely. She hitched up the waist and tugged on her second-best half boots. The next rummage through the drawer, raising a fusty odor, came up with a wool shirt, and she donned that. Now she felt overheated but picked through the jerseys and chose one. She must leave the house or die of heat stroke.

Letty returned, resembling a scarecrow. Woof busily sniffed the clothing. "I need a jersey."

"The bottom drawer."

"Ah, who might these have belonged to?" Letty asked, dragging one on. It, too, fell to her knees. "Somebody really big. A handsome aristocrat, perhaps." Her sister tucked the jersey into the trousers.

"In Grandmother's cottage?" Bia laughed.

"Maybe she hid a notorious French spy."

"Write that down, Letty. Scarves and hats, and we shall venture out."

Letty skipped ahead, Woof followed, down the stairs and to the kitchen. There they found Quinn, the cook and housekeeper. She was relaxed at the worn deal table, sipping a large dish of coffee.

"Gosh a'mighty," she exclaimed. "You two look right peculiar."

"We are going out to cut holly," Letty announced, "and must have a knife."

"Well and good. Take the smallest, and do not hurt yourself." The woman slurped the coffee, a distant look in her eyes. "In the meanwhile, I will think of breakfast. Too early for that, so have a fine time."

"Do you know where there is some holly?" Bia asked.

Quinn waved a hand. "Beyond the rhododendrons. Take care near that gully, you two. Watch your step; it goes right straight down forever. Best stay clear. As I recall, there be a holly bush round there somewheres. Mean to decorate, do you?"

"Some. Letty needs material."

"What say?"

"She wants to mark the holiday," Bia amended.

Letty pulled at her enormous jersey. "Let us go, Bia. Time is flying."

They went to the front door and outside. A gust of frosty air hit their faces.

"Glorious," Letty cried and began to make footprints in the snow. She leaned down and poked in a finger. "Two knuckles, Bia. Two." Woof inspected the resulting hole.

"Very good. Let me carry the knife."

Letty handed it over and ran away, the dog frolicking.

Jeanette Collins

What a daft errand. Bia stuck the short, rather dull knife in the laces of her half boot. Christmas, bah. The spirit had gotten lost. No one was left to celebrate with. Dafter yet, she brooded, to come here to this outpost of humanity, on a whim.

She paced after her sister. Her nose soon became cold, but it was a fine, crisp day, the sky a washed blue. Sunlight slanted through the trees, frost glistening on the bare branches, wood smoke in the air.

"Bia! Bia, come!"

She strolled that direction.

"Quick! Come quick!" Letty shouted.

Bia hurried and found Letty beside a large hump of snow, bending down, and appearing much distressed. "Look, look." She scraped away snow to reveal a brown mane. "It is a horse!"

How strange. "Yes, I can see that."

"Dead." Letty leaned down farther. "Still warm! It melted the snow a little or I would not have seen it in this sort of, um, ditch."

Bia scratched at the itchy jersey and tried to add it up. Had the animal run away? It wore a bridle and a scuffed saddle. Fallen exhausted and died? "Give me that branch, Letty." She tore off dried leaves and, with the stick, cleared snow from around the horse's head and neck.

This exposed matted blood, a lot of it. It had pooled, run down the slope toward the gully, then frozen over. She knelt down, located a gaping wound in the neck, and quickly stood up.

"We must...this animal has been shot!"

Letty just stood there. "Impossible."

"There is a hole in the neck. See? A bullet hole,

4

just like the ducks Daddy used to bring home."

"They had lots of holes."

"This bullet was bigger." She glanced down the slope. "It is a wonder the creature did not fall into that enormous gully. Mercy, Letty, bring the dog."

Letty scooted down the snowy hill toward the ominous crack in the land and caught Woof by the tail. The dog continued digging. To their fresh shock, Woof had uncovered the edge of a tweed coat and a human hand. The whole hillside shifted, and portions began to slide, the snow slowly falling away in a sheet. Letty let go of the dog, which scampered away.

Bia clambered down to help and clutched the cold hand. The two girls strained and grunted, held onto the coat sleeve, then the arm. They grabbed more of the coat and, struggling, hauled the heavy body up the rise. More of the hillside snow soundlessly sank into the abyss. They made it to level ground, helped by the ice and slush. Bia brushed snow from the face of the tall man.

"Oh, horrors, he is hurt. His coat is…" She jumped back, a smear of blood on her hand. Keeping her voice steady, Bia said, "Letty, go fetch Milton and the wood cart. Hurry."

"What for?"

"This man is alive."

Letty ran to find Milton. Woof sat down, his tongue lolling, and looked from the man to Bia and back again.

"Woof, you are a hero," she told the dog, ruffling the shepherd's shaggy fur. "One more minute, and this fellow might have been gone forever."

Bia brushed more snow away from him. He lacked

color, and his breath sounded short. She rubbed her chilly hands together and attempted to warm his face. How long had he been here? Snow had been under him and the horse, so he must have come after it began. From the bloody hole in his coat, his left shoulder was injured. She had the impulse to lie down beside the man, to share her warmth.

Letty raced back. Milton slowly lumbered along, dragging the cart.

"Hurry, Milton," Bia called, "a man is injured."

"I be comin', missy, I be comin'. Little lady here said ye found—erm, crikey." He scowled. "Is he dead?"

"Not yet. Get a move on. I am afraid he has nearly frozen."

"Preserved him like, maybe," Milton opined. "Never care. We will get him back to the cottage." With that, he picked up the body like it weighed nothing and rather dumped it in the cart. Woof jumped in with it, his tail wagging, and the three of them dragged the cart and its burden back up the hill to the house. There, Milton shouted for Quinn, and the three clumsily lugged the man to the kitchen door.

Quinn guarded the way and raised her apron to cover her face. "Do not be bringin' him in here. No, ladies, you must not!"

Bia elbowed her aside. "Rubbish. He is hurt and needs help." They put him on the floor in front of the stove, having no other space big enough. "Milton, go for the doctor."

The gnarled, skinny man objected. "That be about two mile, and then I got to get back again. In the snow," he added for emphasis.

Bia's patience wore thin. "You will go

immediately, Milton, even if there is a blizzard. You are paid to see to our needs, and he has become one of them. Do you want his life on your hands?"

"Oh, missy," he groaned.

"Two shillings if you do it in a hurry," she offered.

Milton hastened out the door, on a mission.

Too late, Bia realized they must now haul the fellow up the stairs. This was too much to attempt. "We will put him in the sitting room, on the sofa, near the fire."

"He is too tall for that," Letty observed.

"We can add the footstool. Quinn, grab his legs."

The woman backed away. "Might be diseased. I haint be touchin' him."

Bia glared at the woman until she relented. Quinn, snorting, took both legs under the knees. She and Letty held his arms. Straining, they got him through the door, across the sitting room, and onto the leather sofa. The snow had melted, and now he was soaking wet.

"These clothes have to go," she decided.

"Outstanding!" Letty cried.

"Not by me!" Quinn declared.

"Then just take the boots. Letty, help me with the coat."

Quinn yanked the boots off, her seamed face guarded. "He be a highwayman, a cutthroat, I wager. You mark my word; he will cause us trouble."

"He will if he dies. Bring me those big scissors. Go!"

They wrestled the coat off him. Quinn brought the scissors and grumbling loudly, hastily left the room. Bia cut the stained shirt away. His left shoulder exposed, they found the wound, a neat round hole. A thin trickle of blood coursed down, possibly from dragging him around. She mopped at it with the shirt.

"Bia," Letty said, "he is bleeding on the sofa from somewhere."

"Get some toweling." She lifted and rolled him slightly. Lord above, the bullet had passed right through! Letty returned with small kitchen towels, and they placed one under him. Bia gently pressed another against the wound. Flaccid, out cold, he did not move or react. Her sister had also brought a length of toweling.

Bia detected a lump on the side of his head and began to panic. He would die here. They would be unable to save him. She put both hands on him and breathed a prayer that he would survive. But he had warmed, his skin was definitely warmer.

"Oh, Bia," Letty whispered, "will he live?"

"Well, he has so far. Call Quinn. We must get the rest of this shirt off."

Shouts and complaints echoed from the kitchen. Quinn appeared at the kitchen door, arms crossed over her outraged bosom. "I will not be undressing this fellow. It is a scandal, and you girls—"

"I absolutely insist!" Bia snapped.

"I will stand here and watch from the door," Quinn announced. "That will be enough."

Bia, afraid the man would bleed to death, clutched the scissors. It must be done. She gathered courage, slowly snipped, and Letty tugged blood-stained pieces away. Now his broad chest, flat belly, and long arms were exposed. Both girls gawked. He had a six-inch or so newly healed cut on his right side, just below his ribs. Golden hair formed a pattern between his brown nipples and trailed down to his trousers.

"Ohhhhh," each of them sighed.

Quinn groaned audibly from the doorway and vanished.

Bia hurried to cover him modestly. If word of this ever got out… "Put the toweling over him, to keep him warm." She stretched the nubbly cloth to hide it all from Letty, who stared.

Now she faced the larger difficulty and took a deep breath. "I will try to get his trousers off."

Letty's green eyes stretched. "Quick, before Quinn comes back."

Bia frowned. "Leave the room, Letty. A child your age has no business—"

Letty stuck out her lower lip. "Balderdash. I need material. When will I ever get this chance again, to see an—um, someone's genuine manhood?"

"Outrageous. With such attitudes, it may happen before you are aware."

"How will you do it?"

Bia clicked the scissor blades. This presented a problem.

"Undo the buttons on his falls," Letty suggested.

"Honestly. I am never letting you out of my sight again, Letty. You have picked up some odd locutions and terms no respectable girl should know."

Letty paid no attention. "Just cut up the legs, and we can pull them off without disturbing him. Go on, Bia, be daring."

Bia steadied herself, reached under the toweling, and undid the falls with shaky fingertips. She began to cut up the outside of the garment, Letty all eyes.

This threatened to expose his long legs.

"Hairy," the girl murmured, studying what she could see. Letty pulled at the bottoms, and off they came, along with his smalls and stockings. Both girls gulped.

Shaken, Bia glanced away. Letty bent over him for a closer inspection. His foot twitched, and she shrieked.

Bia could not help laughing. "The toweling, Letty, you brazen girl." But she could scarcely take her gaze from him. He was beautiful beyond imagination. Stretched out there, insensible, miles tall, his large feet propped on the footstool. He was quite clean, smelled fresh, and his hands were cared for. His hair was sunny blond and rather long. With what they had seen, he was blond all over.

Letty reluctantly covered him. "Is he not a god, Bia? An Apollo? He shall be the gallant duke in my story."

"From that healed cut on his side, I would wager he is a soldier. On his way home from the war."

"The war is over since summer."

"Well, it must take time to sort everyone out."

"He will still be my duke," Letty vowed, touching his bright hair with one finger.

Bia tucked the toweling all around him, uncovered his shoulder, and pressed the cloth against the wound. Blood had accumulated. She folded it over and to quell her fears, made conversation. "Why do you make your stories all about dukes?"

Letty studied the man's feet. "Because they have great power and move my characters around with force. Princes are prisoners of their rank and have no fun. Dukes can do anything they please."

"My, my. Just like certain girls I know." Bia

smoothed his thick, sunlit hair from his forehead. "Look here. Another healed wound on his scalp, hidden by his hair."

Letty bit her thumb. "He is going to be really cross when he finds out we took his clothes and for a minute, looked all over him."

"Then we will not tell him." Bia put another log on the fire. "Blast, where is Milton?"

Letty searched through the pockets of his coat. "He cannot have come far. Why does he not have a heavier coat? And traveling at night, in the snow? Ho, Bia, a money pouch." She shook it. Coins jingled.

"Is there anything else?"

"No. It is a fairly good coat. Maybe he is an émigré. Do Frenchmen wear smalls? That might be a clue."

"Probably they do not. Look at the boots. Are they English?"

Letty lifted one. "I cannot tell." She dropped it with a thud.

The fire spit and crackled. Bia took off her heavy jersey and laid it over him. She put the money pouch and the small knife on the mantel. No holly today. Time passed. Letty was up and down the stairs. Quinn rattled pots in the kitchen. The man's face did not change, but his cheeks had gained a smudge of color.

At last, they heard the muffled noise of horses. Letty ran back as Milton burst in the front door. A small man followed, and they came into the room. He had a somewhat feral face with a long nose and carried a satchel. He took off his hat, revealing a thatch of rust-colored hair. Woof sniffed his boots.

"How do, how do. I am Doctor Fox. Feller here

says you have an injured man."

Letty bit her lips, suppressing a smile.

Bia stepped forward and took his hat. "Thank you for coming, Doctor. We are the Greenways. We found this man, wounded." Bia lifted the cloth, which had become soaked. "Shot, and the bullet traveled through."

The doctor bent over him. "Bring hot water and soap. Clean cloths." He removed his coat, and Letty took it.

"Quinn!" Bia called. "Hot water and soap."

Protests from the kitchen.

"Do I get the two shillings, missy?" Milton inquired.

"Promptly. Go hurry Quinn along with the water. And bring in more firewood."

He moseyed away.

"Fetch more cloths, Letty."

Without ceremony, the doctor stripped the man's entire body of the toweling, shocking Bia, who stepped away but still observed the drama. The doctor explored cautiously and scanned the wound. Bia feared the man would become chilled.

"Missed bone, good. No other injuries. Healthy fellow." He searched all over him with firm fingers. "Healed sword cut, grazed scalp. Hmmmm, soldier, likely. Where are the cloths? Somebody get going!" he yelled.

Letty hurried in with fresh cloths and gaped at the man. Quinn, averting her eyes, carried a pot of water and the soap. The doctor went to work. First, he washed the shoulder front and back, cleaning away streaks of dried blood. Very roughly, in Bia's judgement. He unsnapped his satchel and withdrew a bottle, poured thick, clear liquid on a cloth and cleaned the skin around the wound.

Then some foul-smelling brown paste was spread thickly over the injuries. He folded a clean pad from his case and applied that to the back, then another to the front. Took a roll of coarse linen, lifted the man skillfully, using his knee as a brace, and wrapped it all around the chest and shoulder, to wind up with a compact bandage. Bia hurried to replace the toweling.

The doctor stood straight. "How was this man wounded?"

"We do not know. My sister and I found him this morning, outside, in the snow. His horse was shot dead."

The blighter appeared skeptical. "You did not do it? Lover's quarrel?"

Annoyed, she cried, "Certainly not!"

Letty agreed. "Truly, we never saw him before today."

"Oh, well, had to ask. I will report it to the constable. Now, keep the patient quiet. He must rest and recover. He has lost blood, so give him plenty to eat and drink. I will be out this way tomorrow around this time and have another look." He washed his hands in the cookpot and dried them carefully. "I require one pound, please."

"Well, will he go on bleeding?" Bia asked.

"Not likely, if he remains calm."

"Letty, fetch my reticule."

Letty rushed off, Woof attending.

"New hereabouts, are you?" the doctor asked, putting his things away.

"Yes. We inherited this cottage and property and

came to see about it."

Letty returned, and Bia gave the doctor a sovereign. "Thank you for your care, sir. Um, he will survive?"

He put on his coat and took his crumpled hat. "Unless he develops a fever. Watch out for that. A puzzle for you, eh? Who he might be?"

"We have no idea," Bia told him, "and hope he will tell us. Come back tomorrow. I am worried for him."

"I will be here. Give him that food and drink, when you can. Until then."

He picked up the satchel, replaced his hat, and walked out.

Fever? Not if Bia could help it. No one else was going to die on her.

Bia collected the soiled cloths and took them to the dustbin. Quinn groused over the dirtied pot. Letty brought her notebook and a wooly blanket. The man now was wrapped to his chin, and they sat down before the fire. She scribbled, and Bia considered.

Without a heavier coat, he could not have anticipated a long ride. She did not know the neighborhood well enough to gauge where he might have come from. Or had intended to go. Ashford, the largest village nearby? That was about two miles, as Milton had mentioned. Or Maidstone, but that was even farther, in wintry weather. It was a mystery.

Fidgety, she decided to go out and look again at that horse. Which way had the man been headed? "Letty, I will be back," she said, standing up.

"Where are you going? Quinn is making breakfast."

She retrieved her jumper. "To check that horse

once more."

Letty jumped from her chair. "I will come, too."

Together, they went back out. It had grown colder, and snow had again begun to fall. Fat flakes sat on Bia's face. Woof caught up, and soon they reached the dead horse, which had slid farther down the hill. No way to tell the man's direction. The dog sniffed over the whole area. Bia feared the horse would slide all the way over the brink.

"Quick, Letty, look for a saddlebag or travel bag. Anything to tell us who he is and where he was going."

Woof panted, curious, as the girl kicked away snow, then reached under the horse. "I think something is underneath, Bia."

She knelt down and searched. Went to the other side, felt deeper, moved snow, leaves, and dirt, and caught a canvas strap. She pulled as hard as she could and wrenched it out. Ominously, this disturbed everything. The horse turned, as ice cracked. Rump first, it began to slowly slide down the incline toward the gully.

Bia rolled to the side, nearly losing her grip on the bag. Letty yelped and reached for her. Bia caught onto a rhododendron bush, and the two girls held fast to each other as the horse slipped, slid, and sank into the gully to disappear.

A startling, scary thing! The animal was just plain gone. As the man would have been, and no one would ever have found him. The girls gaped, stunned.

"Oh, Bia. Ghostly."

"Yes, well, um, terrible to see. Just…swallowed up."

"Into the ghastly maw of the earth," Letty

affectedly intoned. "The vengeance of the Furies."

"For what crimes? Fie, now I am all wet."

"Be careful getting up," Letty said, creeping away. "Or else."

Bia crawled after her, dragging the canvas bag. And all this had happened, she mused, before a bite of breakfast.

****

The sisters changed into dry clothes and carried their plates to the sitting room, to observe the patient. They ate, watching the man carefully. Bia returned the dishes to the kitchen.

Quinn raved. "Goin' to be trouble, mind you, miss. No way your grandmama would have let a strange man into the house, God rest her. No indeed."

"Then whose clothes did we put on?" Bia asked.

Quinn did not answer but went on scrubbing a skillet. "Do best to sell this place, I say. Get your money out and ride back to Dover. I be goin' to my auntie in Hythe. She be sixty years old and needs me. I will not be settin' here this next year, mark my word. No, I tell you, not with no company but Milton. By the by, he wants his two shillings, miss."

"I will give it to him. Is the coffee done?"

"Sure, it always be done. Help yourself."

Bia carried two cups back to the sitting room to find Letty peering under the blanket.

"Disgraceful girl!" she scolded. "Have you no shame?"

"He will never know. I required a measurement."

"Put that cover back instantly," Bia ordered, "and take this coffee."

Letty accepted the cup. "I used my notebook as a

16

you ruffian. It cost me money to rescue you, and I intend to have it back."

Surprised, he then had the nerve to laugh, a rumble in his chest. "I will reimburse your costs, ma'am." His gaze cold, he added, "Do not be a thief for tuppence."

"Worthless coins, I take it? Like your manners."

Letty came back with a plate piled high. "Here we are. Quinn's best whipped eggs and ham. And a muffin."

Of a sudden, he showed great interest in the food. His blue eyes caught the light as he balanced the plate and began to eat voraciously. The girls observed this, as did Woof. He ate the muffin in two bites. He chewed, regarded the dog, speared a clump of egg, and flipped it. Woof jumped up and caught it in his mouth. Letty clapped her hands, the dog visibly amazed.

Bia could not take her eyes from him. He made no move to cover himself but sat there bare to the waist. The colors of him, his sunny hair and summer sky eyes. The warm tones of his skin. His liquid muscles.

He coughed and tried to clear his throat.

"Letty, bring water."

The girl darted away. Woof sat poised in case anything else delicious flew his direction. Back Letty came, took the empty plate, and gave him the glass, her face worshipful. He drank it and appeared energized.

"Again, I am grateful. My sincere thanks. I am a good deal better. If I could have my clothes, I will take myself off."

Letty quickly left with the dishes.

Bia spoke. "I am afraid we rather laid waste to those. You were covered in ice and snow, and your things got all wet. Soooo…we had to cut them off.

Your boots are all right."

This got his attention. He squinted. "What do you mean, we?"

"It is of no consequence. We will find you something to wear."

He fixed her with his gaze. "Everything went with the horse?"

"No, we found a canvas bag. Under the horse, then it slid right into—"

He lifted a long arm, the hand she had caught hold of outstretched. "Give it to me!"

"Do you do nothing but issue orders?" she crossly replied. "It is right here, and no, we did not open it or take anything. As for that, I will be surprised if you can stand up on your own. A night in the snow and considerable blood loss have surely taken a toll."

"Well…"

"It has grown late for travel. Have a night's rest. Your horse is in the depths of Hades for all we know. And it snowed again. I do question how you look out for yourself, gadding about the countryside without a suitable coat."

Letty returned, easing into the room. "Did you tell him, Bia?" she whispered.

"More or less."

"Oh, grand." Letty dragged her chair closer to him, her notebook and pencil in hand. "Tell us now, sir, how did you get that sword cut we chanced to see on your side? And what happened to your head?"

He smiled affably. "You wielded the scissors, I take it, little miss?"

"I helped. Were you in the war?"

"Everyone was in the war. Were you offended by

my scars?"

"Mercy, no. Nothing offends me. I am a writer and want to observe life in the raw."

"Huh. I have some of it, if your mama will allow."

Letty giggled. "Oh, silly. Bia is my sister."

He feigned disbelief. "Really? I could have sworn. She is so stern a lady. However, a mite too pretty to be old."

"Yes, everyone says so. Bia was the belle of Dover."

"Letty, stop your stories," she warned.

Her sister dramatically lifted her hand. "Every ship that sailed had officers on the deck calling out for Beautiful Bianca to wave them away."

"Invent something else, you scamp," Bia said. "She makes all this up, you know."

"It is not true?" he asked.

"It is!" Letty insisted. "Daddy said so. Our father, Captain Elijah Greenway of the Royal Navy," she bragged, "was harbormaster of Dover Port."

"I am honored to be in such distinguished company." He wearily passed his hand across his face.

Bia stood. "You are very tired. If you wish to try, we can help you upstairs, and you may rest in a better bed."

"Yes, we can do that," Letty agreed.

"What about my…" His voice trailed off.

"Just um, wrap the blanket around you."

He got to his feet, grasping the blanket. Letty helped hold the blanket up and put her arm around his waist. Bia did the same. He put his good arm over her shoulders and squeezed. Almost a hug, but she might have imagined it. Slowly, very slowly, they made their way from the sitting room to the stairs and started up.

Finding the staircase too narrow for three, Letty went ahead. Bia took his weight as she was able. They haltingly made it up, step by step, his arm close around her. She smelled his hair and skin, perspiration, and horseflesh. A tremor passed over her spine, an awareness. When she glanced up at his face, he looked down at her, his blue eyes questioning.

They reached the landing as Letty ran ahead to the third chamber and lit the lamps. Bia got him down the hall to the spare room and the bed. Letty turned back the cover. He sat down, breathing hard, the blanket around him. Bia gazed at his knees, fuzzy blond calves, and remarkable feet.

"That was a trek. I do thank you, ladies. I am ever in your debt."

"We will leave you to be comfortable. Another blanket is there. If you require anything, call out. I hope you can rest."

Bia left the room and, in the hall, waited. Letty quietly asked, "So what was it? Some awful Frenchman cut your side?"

She flattened to the wall, listening.

"A soldier just tried to save himself. Go along, Miss Letty. I am a tired man."

"Never mind. Rest. We will talk later."

"My hearty thanks. And to you, too, Miss Bianca," he called.

Bia blushed hotly as Letty sauntered from the room and closed the door. "Is he not splendid, Bia?" she whispered excitedly.

She propelled her sister back to the stairs. "He can fill whole pages. But tomorrow, he will be gone. We had no lunch. It must be time for tea, do you not think?"

Chapter Two

Adrian got himself under the covers, tired to the bones. He touched a sore place on the side of his head. Must have hit something when he fell. It ached, but his shoulder burned like fire. Very tired. How had he gotten here? Battered from the crossing, exhausted. Dover in the rain. The inn, then the letters. He had to get home!

Someone had tried to kill him. Did nothing ever end? If not for those two girls…too worn-out to think. Horse gone, but they had saved the bag. He could make it. Just a little rest. Just an hour…

A sound woke him. He lay still as a figure moved toward him in the low light. Her. Bianca. Adrian braced himself. If she tried anything, he was ready. She placed a carafe of water and a glass on the bedside table and just stood there, gazing down at him. A long moment passed. Then she tucked the blanket closer around him, covered him with another, and silently withdrew.

Adrian breathed again, touched by her kindness. Tears welled up; it had been so long, her womanly caring, her gentle hand. The years of suffering and death weighed him down, the pain, the desperation and futility. Must hang on. Out of it now. It was over, it must be over. He could do no more. Get home, rest, see what was what.

He forced himself to relax. Still alive, damn them.

After everything, he lived. His thoughts spiraled, he closed his eyes, and slept.

****

The rest of the afternoon went by without a sound from him. After dinner, Letty went off to her room to write. Bia bid good night to Quinn, who also retired. She returned to the sitting room, put her sewing away, and straightened up. Folded the man's ruined clothing but did not throw it out. They had not learned his name.

She longed to have another look at him. It had all been somewhat unreal, finding him in the snow, lugging him home. Obviously, he was a vigorous man. If he had his clothes, he might have tried to leave, horse or no. But he was worn flat, she had seen that. Likely, tired for a long time. He was very lean, not to say thin. His ribs had been visible, his belly flat, as though he had missed quite a few meals. The war had taken everything. Poor fellow.

Bia went to the kitchen, fetched a little jug of water and a glass, and climbed the stairs. She listened at his door. Silence, so she opened it and tiptoed in. Yes, there he lay, quite actual, fast asleep. She put the water and glass on the bedside table and stood back, barely able to see him in the dim light. How superb a man, healthy, young, and alive. Old dreams unfolded in her head, rose up into citadels, then died again, as they had died before.

She gazed down at him, longing blankly for what might be called hope. For sorrow to get tired of her, for memories to lose substance. For some kind of peace and acceptance. They would come, but it might take time. Perhaps more time than she had. She added the other blanket, turned, and silently left the room.

****

Wednesday

Bia and Letty made it downstairs to breakfast at about the usual time. They sat down to eggs and more of the ubiquitous ham which appeared daily in one form or another. This monotony was only relieved by a variety of muffins Quinn was expert at. Today's sported strawberry jam in the middle and was quite tasty.

Woof politely sat beside Letty's chair, his molasses-brown eyes moving from her plate to her mouth.

"Is the man all right, do you suppose, Bia?"

"He seemed extremely tired. I am glad he can sleep. We will leave him alone."

Letty ate the inside of her muffin. "But what if he needs to get up?"

"I left the chamber pot beside his bed."

"Mark my word, I will not be cleaning up no strange man's leavings, uh-uh," Quinn announced.

Letty kept eating. Bia did not react.

The woman frowned, making crooked furrows in her forehead. "No, ma'am, or I be leaving right this day. I got all I can do."

"Quitting so near payday?" Bia mildly inquired. "Losing your wages does seem a shame."

Palpable rage filled the room. Quinn raised her ample bosom menacingly, her lips a thin line.

"Might I have more of your delicious coffee?" Bia asked.

The cook poured.

Letty tossed a bit of egg to Woof. He missed, skidded over it with his paws, searched all about, then eagerly licked the tile floor.

Quinn groaned.

****

Fresh snow had fallen. Letty skipped about. "More snow, Bia. It never snowed in Dover."

Nothing would satisfy but they must go out. The girls crept upstairs for the old clothes, changed, and met in the hallway. They listened at the man's door but heard nothing, so went back down and outside.

Milton was in the back yard cutting firewood and stacking it in the shed. Woof ran around, tossing up snow with his nose.

Milton stopped work and waggled his bushy brows. "Do not be goin' near that gully again. It sucks in little ladies as yerself."

"We know this," Letty related. "It gobbled up that entire horse."

"Did that, ye say?" he asked, testing the saw edge with a calloused thumb.

"Go back there and see, Milton. The animal is gone."

Bia examined the leaves of the rose bushes, which were coated in ice. Would they bloom again?

"It be the curse workin'," Milton pronounced.

Letty stopped dead. "What curse?"

"The white lady. She comes when it snows, steals young children, and takes 'em down there with her. Into the gully."

"What for?"

Milton hefted another log. "How would I be knowin'?"

"That is just a cautionary tale, Milton," Letty instructed the man. "To scare children, so they do not go around there."

"I reckon she eats 'em. Wal, I got to saw this wood."

They walked around to the other side of the house. Here the snow was deeper.

"We can make a snowman!" Letty formed a snowball, put it on the ground, and began to roll it into a bigger shape. "Make another, Bia."

The two worked over the snow until they had two good-sized balls. Now they had to lift one to put it on top of the other.

"Do no more, Letty. We must lift the smaller one."

They grappled with this, but it broke in half and fell.

"Blast," Bia complained. "The snow is too soft."

"I am tired of this, Bia. My fingers are cold."

"So much for a frost fair. Let us go around front and see if—"

The two stopped in surprise when a large man on horseback appeared out of the pine grove, observed them, and rode their way. Woof made garbled sounds in his throat and raised one front paw. Bia eyed the rider. Milton was nearby; they could call for him if needed. She would brazen it out and stepped forward.

"Good day, sir," she confidently stated.

He touched his hat. "Good day, ladies."

"Where are you bound in such weather?" she questioned.

"Not far, ma'am." He smiled, but it was not friendly. "I seek a fellow traveler. Has anyone come by? Last night? I lost track of him in the storm."

"Mercy, no," Letty swiftly said. "Nobody ever comes this way, off the main road. Where do you hail from?"

"Not far," he repeated.

Bia reckoned he had lost interest in them, but he asked again, his tone suspicious. "You have seen no one, you say?"

"In the last week, only you," she confirmed.

Without another word, he turned his mount and rode back into the wood. Letty ran to see where he went, but he was already out of sight. She strolled back, and the two retraced their steps, Milton still sawing logs. They kicked snow off their boots and went into the kitchen, passed Quinn stirring a pot, and hurried to the sitting room fire.

Letty warmed her hands, and Bia took off the itchy jersey. Woof lay down on the hearth.

"A rough fellow, eh, Bia?"

"He did not seem sociable. I would not have told him the correct time of day."

The girl considered this. "He was looking for our guest."

"Who else?"

"Not a constable," Letty mused, "but he had a Baker rifle in his saddle scabbard."

"I saw it. We must talk to our patient. He is running from trouble, as Quinn said. Out traveling in the dark, with no heavy coat."

"We cannot wake him up to ask," Letty said.

"No need," came a deep voice from the stairs.

They turned, and there he stood, blanket and all, his tousled blond hair golden as the sun.

****

Adrian had heard their voices below his window, sat up a little, and looked out. There were the girls, dressed in an assortment of clothing. Playing in the snow, making a snowman. Uh-oh, it fell.

A movement caught his eye. *Jesus, who is that?* He pulled himself up and put his ear closer to the window casement. The man spoke, and Adrian caught a few words. "...seeking a traveler, lost track...."

The girl, Letty, fended him off with a lie, and her sister, Bianca, agreed to it. The man rode away. He had to leave here, or they might get hurt. But he had no clothes. *Where is the bag?* Downstairs. He swung his legs out of bed. His shoulder, stiff to the waist, pained him but felt no worse. Starved, his belly pinched. Must get away. If they had a horse, he would steal it. Pay them back later.

He managed to stand, wavered, wrapped the blanket around his middle, and made it to the door. Opened it and a wave of dizzy nausea overwhelmed him. He leaned on the jamb to catch his breath. Moved along the wall to the stairs and started down, toward their light voices.

They wanted answers and feared to wake him. He took a long breath and said, "No need."

The two rushed to his side.

"Are you foolish?" Bianca asked. "You might have fallen."

"My clothes. In the bag."

"Yes, come, sit down."

They supported him to a chair by the fire. He dragged his steps and had barely enough strength to hold onto the damn blanket. "I am quite done in. I do apologize."

"Poor dear," Letty sympathized. "I will go and get your food." She rushed away.

Bia called after her sister, "Send Quinn to help,"

and brought the canvas bag. "You are weak, sir, and must rest. Clothing is in here?"

"Yes."

The older woman did not come. The girl hesitated, then decided.

She unbuckled the bag and extracted his flannel shirt, trousers, stockings, and smalls. What a courageous girl. Young, unmarried, virginal. Must have been shocked by him. She helped him into the loose shirt, a small agony to raise his arm. But her hands were gentle as she buttoned it, careful of his wound.

"The dressing is clean," she observed.

She knelt down to help with his stockings. Quickly, she edged the blanket aside and added the smalls, drawing them to his knees.

He was mortified. "I can manage," he offered.

"Hush."

One foot, then the other in the legs. She deftly worked first the smalls, then the trousers up his legs. Adrian stood again, shaky, gripping the blanket. He held onto her fine shoulders, and she arranged the clothes on him. His unfortunate cock was too tired to take proper notice of a woman's hands. She swiftly buttoned the falls, not touching his skin, her gaze elsewhere, and he sat down heavily.

She smiled like a goddess. Adrian took the moment to really look at her face and form. Her glossy, reddish brown hair was piled up in waves on her head. Clear skin, straight nose, green eyes, full, rosy mouth. Tall enough, slender, and as ripe as a berry. The look-alike younger sister, the writer, returned with food. His stomach clenched.

"There," Bia said. "We will consider the boots

later."

"Now you must eat." Letty smiled, holding out the steaming plate. "Quinn says she will not do more, Bia."

Bia frowned, but said, "We will manage."

Grateful, he said, "Thank you, both of you. For everything."

"Just eat."

Bianca, he thought, scooping up eggs and ham. Italian, meaning white, fair. He bit into a tasty muffin filled with jam, his gaze on them. They seemed innocent as doves, but they had lied to the intruder. Allies, perhaps. He cleaned the plate, the brown and white shepherd dog's eyes on him.

"Sorry, Wolf," he said. "I forgot you."

"Not wolf," Letty corrected. "His name is Woof, like the bark. Because he does not. Bark, that is. He barely growls, like he did when that man came," she added, her intelligent glance vigilant. "But I imagine you saw him?"

"I did. You are a deuced clever girl, Miss Letty."

"I knew it," she gloated, "or you would not have got out of your bed."

Bia left with his plate.

"I can describe him," the girl said. "I have a mind for detail. He was big, had a rough, craggy sort of face, and a coarse manner, though he tried to speak like a gentleman. He had a rifle in his scabbard. Not a constable, though. They always say so. We think he was looking for you. Claimed to have—"

"Thank you, I heard most of what he said."

Bia brought him a cup of coffee. He began to adore her.

"He wore a heavy coat," Letty went on, "and a sort

of uniform or livery under it."

His heart stopped. "What color?"

"Dark blue. A gold-trimmed, stand-up collar."

Adrian's mind crowded with questions. Who the hell was after him? He had not recognized the man, but the blue and gold livery struck a familiar chord. He must get moving but had no strength. Could he risk another day here? Would they have him?

He drank the coffee, working it out. The two girls were waiting. He had to tell them something, but how much?

"I owe you an explanation, ladies, but confess to be somewhat in the dark myself. I have, shall we say, suffered some losses. I am caught up in a situation that requires care."

"Just tell us how you got here," Letty offered.

"Where you were coming from," Bia added.

Adrian considered this and arranged the story. "I was in the army and wounded at the siege of Hougoumont Chateau, part of the battle of Waterloo."

The girls paid rapt attention. He went on.

"By the time help got to me, I was feverish, delirious, all that. I was taken with others to a hospital tent, then on to Brussels.

"Inconveniently, I could not remember who I was. The doctor said I had suffered a concussion and must wait until the swelling subsided, then, um, perhaps. To shorten the yarn, my memory gradually returned, and I eventually recovered enough to be discharged from duty. A few days ago, I got out of bloody Belgium and took ship home."

He stopped to catch his breath and finished the coffee. "Look in the bag, Bianca. The packet of papers.

That is me, who I am. After five years away, I have lately discovered the world thinks me dead. I must put my life back together."

Bia did not reach for the papers. "We can take your word, sir."

"We believe you," said faithful Letty. "That fellow cannot find you; woods surround this property. Not a trace of your horse remains, and we told that fellow lies. I should have directed him to the gully and given him a push. He shot you, I think, then came back to find you and make sure you were dead."

"But why?" Bianca asked.

He revealed more. "I received overdue letters when finally discharged. In Dover, I took a room at an inn, rested a little, and read them. Suffice to say, my affairs are in a snarl. I am trying to get home to straighten it all out."

"You rode from Dover?" she asked. "That is near twenty miles."

"I made good time and stopped at a hedge tavern along the way. I uh, suspected I might have been followed from the inn. I hung my coat by the door and sat in an out-of-the-way corner. In five minutes, he came in."

"Who?" Letty inquired.

"The same man you spoke to outside. He recognized my coat hanging there and went to have a pint. My suspicion confirmed, I hustled out a side door."

"That is why you had no coat," Letty excitedly said.

"Yes. I tried to lose him. Then it began to snow, heavily for a time. I left the road and wove back and forth through the trees. I heard the shot, the horse went down, and I jumped away. Hit my head and have no more recollection until I woke here." He pinned them with a glance. "Who exactly took my clothes?"

"I did," Bia confessed.

"I helped," Letty insisted.

Startling. "Is there no man about?"

"Only Milton, our man-of-all-work," Bia answered. "He went for the doctor."

"He does not do anything in the house but bring in wood. Milton helped get you up the hill from the infamous gully in the wood cart," Letty explained. "It is haunted by the white lady, he said, who eats children."

"The wood cart?" he joked.

Letty shook with laughter. "No, the gully."

"Where is your home?" Bia asked, obviously wanting more information.

He must not say too much, or ruin everything. "Near Ashford. I nearly made it." But somebody wanted me never to arrive, he added to himself. The women gazed at him with trust. He had told them enough for the present. Christ crucified; his whole arm throbbed.

"I do not suppose," he queried, "that you have any spirits?"

"Quinn does, I saw it." Letty hastened away.

Bianca, the practical one, studied him. "Your shoulder pains you."

"Most perceptive, ma'am."

"You ought to lie down."

"Yes." He sighed deeply. Would that the beautiful Bianca would lie with him.

Letty raced back with a large, half-filled bottle. "I

had to tussle with Quinn to get it. She called it her heart medicine, but it is brandy." She tipped some into a glass and handed it to him. He drank it right down.

Bia wanted to hear his story. "Give him more, Letty." He would get sozzled and talk, Bia reasoned. His story seemed spotty to her. He had not told all. He drank the liquor without cringing, and Letty poured more, her eyes wide with interest. He swallowed that, too.

Now his posture eased. He handed back the glass, moved his left arm, supported it with the other hand, and stood up. Bia rose from her chair and guided him to the sofa. Letty moved the footstool closer to support his feet as he lay back. Woof hopped up, rested his paws on the leather, and panted. The dog seemed to approve and jumped down again to sit by Letty's chair.

Bia covered him with the blanket and met his eyes. She felt drawn into the blue depths and glanced away.

"Woof never barks?" he asked.

"No," she answered.

"We found him on the docks," Letty replied. "In a mess, all wet and muddy. He had no fat on him at all; his bones poked out. And he was heartbroken that nobody wanted him. Daddy said we could keep him. We fed him lots, groomed and petted him, and now he is happy again. We do not need him to bark. He knows we love him, just as he is."

Woof's tail thumped the floor.

"More brandy?" Bia inquired. She held out his glass.

His winning smile. "Heart medicine, Miss Bianca?"

"A cure-all perhaps." She poured out a substantial

amount. "Are you willing to tell us your name?"

He hesitated for a fraction. "Adrian."

She caught the delay. Letty quickly wrote that down in her notebook. Now he sipped the liquor. His eyes became merry; he relaxed further. *Ah*, Bia thought, *he is halfway gone*.

"Now," Letty said, "about that sword cut."

"Bloodthirsty girl." He chuckled. "A pirate queen."

"I need material."

As Bia studied him, he glanced away, seemed to think it over, then began to talk.

"Very well. My last duty. I was among officers serving Lieutenant Colonel James Macdonell. He had assumed command of Hougoumont and the various brigades defending the property." Adrian could still see and smell it, the wet earth, the rotting, fallen apples.

"The chateau was more a large farmhouse with outbuildings, orchards, and woods, ringed by a wall. We were ordered to hold the position against whatever came. It rained, then rained some more. We used everything available to us and barricaded the house. Took up vantage points and, through the night, drank gin and ate soggy bread to keep awake.

"We were well positioned to act mainly as a diversion. The plan was to divide French attention and draw troops away from activity occurring farther along the road. Wellington had moved in massive forces, and a great conflict loomed; everyone knew. I could feel it in the air, a hellish sort of heat. We were to join them in the field but came under heavy attack."

He paused and drank. "Saturday dawned. The battle, now known as Waterloo, started about eleven in the morning with a sustained cannon barrage. Fighting began in the orchard and woods. Hundreds of men stormed through our defenses and tried to take the walls." Again, he halted, remembering the horror.

"It became a slaughter. Riflemen stationed on firing platforms cut down the French in droves. Still they came, trying to breach the walls and cross an open area to reach the chateau buildings."

He shook his head sadly. "They fell like colorful birds, but there were more to take their places. Our men dropped back to the barricaded house, under cannon fire.

"We were soon mobbed by what seemed thousands of French troops. We continued to hold them off. After some hours, they laid siege to the north gate, the only one not heavily barricaded. This had been used for resupply and communication. And as an escape route, if everything went wrong. It was too late for that. At all costs, it must be kept closed, and we bent to this effort. The French came at it with everything they had, and the gate was finally battered open."

He paused, the recollection so vivid, he heard the clamor and smelled the charred air. "Many French broke through." He emptied the glass.

"I and other men joined the colonel and, fighting hand to hand, closed the gate again. The Frenchmen trapped inside fell to the sword. In the skirmish, a ball caught the top of my head, grazing my scalp. My helmet flew off; blood gushed into my eyes. I staggered. A chap swept out with his sword and slashed through my coat. I fell among the dead."

Bia and Letty were transfixed, and he smiled impishly.

"So, Miss Letty, that is how I got that sword cut."

Bia held out the brandy bottle. "Have more." He presented his glass, and this time, she filled it to the top.

By God, the girl aimed to get him sloshed. Little did she know how much liquor he could put away. He drank it gladly. It numbed his pain.

It marked the first occasion Adrian had told his story in any sort of order. It had taken him some days to connect events. After a time, his head cleared, and he read the news accounts. The papers passed among the men until they were in tatters. The Battle of Waterloo had gone on through the following day, Sunday, June eighteenth, to bring a resounding defeat to that pretentious swine, Napoleon. Colonel Macdonell had survived, he read, as had valiant James Graham and other brave officers and men.

Adrian tried diligently to recall comrades he had seen go down in the battle. To honor them by remembering their names and faces. His recollections of the encounter remained tenuous. He had a scar on his head and felt beaten all over with a stick. Meanwhile, his right flank was stitched up. Dosed with laudanum, he lay in bed until his side had healed enough not to release the precious contents therein. He had by now lost so much weight thanks to a lingering fever, extra portions of food were given him. He ate anything offered to gain back his strength, which had been damn slow in coming.

And all that time, the hospital tent was being slowly dismantled around him and other soldiers of the king. Everyone wanted to go home to England as soon as they got to their feet, and so did he. Adrian now felt marooned and forgotten. More time passed. He was weak, badly slowed down, and everything took forever.

His dissatisfaction grew every hour. He fought against despair. If he did not get out of this bind, he would run mad. Finally, he cranked up an illusion of health and faked his way out of the collapsing unit.

Eventually, he faced a battle-ravaged major who gave him ten seconds of sympathy and his discharge papers from the celebrated Second Coldstream Regiment of Guards. He was also given a draft for back pay, two stained and mud-smeared letters, and a ticket that would get him home. Along with his field bag, he had his pouch with ten gold British sovereigns, and some loose francs. Adrian was free, though somewhat diminished.

His showy uniform, sword, and pistol were long gone, and he was in donated rags. He purchased clothing that almost fit from a street peddler. In another day, Adrian traveled to Ostend in a hired carriage with three other wounded officers, every jolt in the road a heavy blow for them. They took ship in a rainstorm. Lightning cracked over the little vessel, and Adrian began to worry the gods were against him as he clung to a railing. After all his difficulties, would he drown in the cold sea? Many were sickened, but Adrian held onto whatever he ate, too hungry to let it come back up.

After two stormy days of being steadily tossed around the ocean, they made it to Dover. He and others nearly fell off the ship to solid ground, heartily grateful to have survived. With what strength Adrian possessed, he found a room in a nearby inn and slept until he had to get up and eat. He stuffed himself with food and slept some more.

Then he read the two letters and was stricken to the heart. No more time to rest here. Must head home at once! He washed and dressed and left the inn. With so many soldiers about, no hired carriage could be had. At a stable, Adrian paid for a half-decent horse and saddle and began the journey to Ashford, traveling as fast as he could.

And here he was with these two women. Ladies, to be plain, who had saved his life.

****

Bia remained uncertain what to think of this man, Adrian. The things he said had the ring of truth. His features were openly honest, and she had seen his wounds, new and old. There would be scant reason to invent such a story. It must all have happened as he said. Letty scribbled in her notebook, the tip of her tongue between her teeth.

Quinn edged around the door, her expression guarded. "I fixed soup," she announced. "If anybody is eating today." She took a few steps into the room, twisting her apron strings, to view him. "So. You be better?"

"I am, thank you, ma'am. Helped by your excellent food. That was a superior jam muffin."

Quinn, perplexed by this gentlemanly show of manners, retreated to the kitchen.

"You wait there," Letty said. "We will bring your food." She skipped away.

Alone with him, Bia was embarrassed for reasons she could not quite fathom. Knowing his story, watching him speak, had almost been too much to bear. He had suffered. It was hugely intimate. And she had seen him naked. Briefly. Had touched his skin. Too much knowledge to carry, and now where would she put it? She'd had enough; her head was full. She quickly stood. "I will help with lunch."

"Bianca," he said, "I hope I have not burdened you too much with my problems."

Blast, he reads minds. "I am glad you can talk about it. That you can accept what occurred and are not bitter."

"How can I be? I lived. Many did not."

"But the *uselessness* of it all," she lamented. "The terrible waste!" To her dismay, tears gathered in her throat.

He gazed at her with great concentration. "Ohhhh. I see. You lost someone."

Bia rushed away. In the kitchen, she arranged cheese and apples on a plate.

"Potato and ham soup," Quinn announced, filling bowls.

Bia and Letty exchanged weary looks.

"Ham's been right good this fall," Quinn boasted. "Got us a big one." The woman gestured with her thumb. "Now we be feedin' himself in there. And folks eatin' all over the house will draw mice."

"Woof will catch them," Letty allowed, "and gnaw them down to their tiny bones."

Woof panted in agreement. Quinn vigorously stirred her mixing bowl. The girls ferried dishes to the sitting room and distributed them about.

Letty gave Adrian a bowl of soup, a spoon, and a serviette. She laid another serviette over his chest. "Are you comfortable, Adrian?" she affectionately asked.

His smile seemed to light the room. "With your kind care, Miss Letty, I am prospering."

Mercy, Bia thought, *he must leave before they all go overboard for him.* She spooned up the soup, which was good. Quinn must have bought the whole pig. Sausages might come next. Her glance strayed to him. How excessively tall he was. How glorious his golden hair. His hands….

How could a man be so beautiful? Never mind the things he must have done in the army to stay in one attractive piece.

Letty, never still for long, began to talk.

"We came up here from Dover," she related. "Our grandmother left us this cottage, and we thought we might live here. Otherwise, it has been suggested we go to Italy. Our mama was Italian, you know. She died when I was ten. I imagine it is where I got my love of literature."

"Who suggested we go to Italy, Letty?" Bia inquired.

"Well, I did. Why not? My name is Violetta," she told him, "but no one calls me that. When I publish my book, it will say 'Violetta Greenway' on the spine." She measured the statement with two fingers. "In gold letters."

"That will leave no room for the title," Bia joked, offering Adrian the cheese plate.

He took a chunk and asked, "What shall your book be about, Letty?"

"A powerful duke and his adventures. He has three mistresses, and that leads to trouble. Then his wicked uncle tries to steal the one he likes best, and he has to go after her. To Scotland, maybe. When he leaves, the other two have a duel over him."

His expressive brows lifted. "Dueling mistresses! What a fellow this must be. Then what happens?"

"I have not written that far yet. I am still trying to

flesh out the duke. Now that you have come, Adrian, I am going to write you in."

"Not as the wicked uncle, I trust. Nor the runaway mistress, I beg of you."

"No, no, you shall be the duke."

"A rise in rank to be sure. I am flattered."

"Dukes have all the fun," Letty insisted. "They have great power."

He sighed. "I can attest to that."

It made a merry time. "I do not know how you come to all this, Letty." Bia laughed. "We do not know a single duke."

"But you knew James, and he was a viscount."

Bia picked up dishes and left the room. Letty could *never* be silent.

"Oh, Bia, I am sorry!" her sister called. "Do come back!"

But Bia went to the kitchen and would not hear her.

Adrian listened to the sisters. *James, eh? Threw her over? Is that why Bia's sad? Because she is. A ring of sorrow is in the iris of her green eyes.* She was quite beautiful, so this James might have been a bounder and bruised her tender feelings. He framed a question for her sister, but Letty, the talker, told him.

"Bia had a beau," she confided in a low voice. "Lieutenant Viscount James Frazer-Griffin of the Royal Marines, an artillery officer. He went away."

Jesus, a sailor. "Did he not return?" Adrian asked.

Now Letty became sad. It was like watching the loft go out of a hot air balloon. She just deflated. "Yes. They brought him back. But they should not have." She dropped her voice further. "There was little left of him. He did not know her, but Bia sat with him in the hospital for three days and nights until his family came. And then he died. Do not breathe that I told you."

"I promise. When did this happen?"

"A year ago, last October. But then, right after all that, Daddy died, too. Then last spring, our grandmama went. Everything seemed to be falling apart. Suddenly, we were orphans."

How hard for them. "All in this last year or so?" he asked, wanting to hear more.

"Yes. We were desperate for a time, all on our own. But Bia is a tower of strength and kept everything together. She is wonderful, you know. So brave and good, and very smart and pretty."

Letty petted Woof, her sharp gaze on him. "You are not married, are you?"

"No."

She smiled prettily. "And a good thing. Think what a ruckus your wife would raise, you alone here with a lady as wonderful as Bia."

Adrian had to admire her, so full of sparks. "Mischievous girl. How old are you?"

"Sixteen. Bia is almost twenty. And you?"

"Five and twenty."

"Hmmmm. Not too old."

"But a little beaten up?"

"It does not show," she earnestly said. "Only your intimates will know."

Intimates, yet. Adrian laughed out loud.

Chapter Three

Bia busied herself in the kitchen. Quinn had baked cakes for tea. The cook mixed icing in a saucer, then drizzled it over the cakes. Bia put them on a pretty plate. The treats, she knew, were to impress Adrian. Let a man come around, Letty went into a lather, and something other than ham might be served at dinner.

Mysteriously, he had not disclosed his last name. A jealous husband after him? Not realistic. And who would have come back, like that fellow this morning? A person hired to do evil? A desperate enemy? A Frenchman, seeking revenge? Really, she was as fanciful as Letty.

She probably should go back before her sister told all the family secrets. Bia drifted to the sitting room, but all was quiet. Letty busily wrote in her notebook, and Adrian slept. She sat, took up her embroidery, threaded her needle, and allowed herself to regard him. She could look at him for days and might have to, if he did not recover and go away. If he lived near Ashford, he might come back for a visit. Lunacy, why would he? *He had better repay the expenses*, she irritably thought.

A knock at the front door so alarmed the girls, they both jumped up.

"I will go," Bia said.

"Maybe it is that man with the rifle," Letty whispered.

"Wait here." She strolled to the front door and opened it, ready for anything. Doctor Fox brushed past her.

"Afternoon," he said, handing her his battered hat. "How is he?"

She closed the door. "Um, doing well, we think. He slept, ate, and drank. He has not complained much. I gave him some brandy."

"Will do no harm," he said, pacing into the sitting room.

Adrian was awake and sat up.

"Greetings, young feller," Fox boomed. "How are ye?"

"Well enough, sir. You are the doctor?"

"Doctor Fox, my lad. Let me have a look." He removed his coat to reveal a gaily striped calico shirt.

The man fairly yanked at Adrian's buttons, rudely removed half the shirt, unwound his handiwork, and exposed the area.

Letty hovered so closely, the doctor frowned threateningly. She stepped back, all eyes.

Bia thought him a savage, but the injury looked exceptionally good. The redness had disappeared. The skin all around the wounds appeared healthier. To her, it was miraculous. There was no sign of the smelly brown paste.

"Right good," he pronounced. "I believe you will live, ho ho. I will bandage this up again, then perchance you could visit my office after the holiday? Say, on the coming Tuesday?"

Adrian shifted his position, obviously uncomfortable. Bia's heart twitched. *How brave he is!*

"Where are you located, sir?"

"Number Seven Ashford High Street."

"What happened to Doctor Knowles?" he asked, some concerned.

"Retired last year, when I came. Still in his old location, if you want him. Good town, Ashford." Out came the nasty paste, and he applied more, front and back, repeated his complex bandaging, and briskly pulled down the shirt. "That will be one pound."

Bia counted out shillings from her reticule and handed them to him. Letty helped Adrian with his shirt sleeve.

"Thank you, miss." He turned to Adrian. "I informed Constable Fugate of this incident; that is the law. Said I would and I did. He had the notion it was a poacher's stray shot. Poachers, said I! At night? In the snow? So watch your step out there. Who shot you?"

"I do not yet know."

"Hmmm. Take care. Somebody might have more naughtiness in mind. Well, I am off. Rest, eat, drink, and see me next week. Ta-ta."

He collected his hat and satchel and marched out. Bia helped Adrian right his shirt buttons again.

"He resembled a fox," Adrian remarked, leaning back on the sofa.

"We thought so, too," Letty agreed.

"He is a trifle humorous," Bia agreed, "but your injury is doing well."

Adrian gazed into her eyes. "Now I owe you two pounds. Hand me the money pouch."

Bia shook her head. "I cannot take it. You have no horse, no coat, and you are stranded here, injured. Just get better. You then have to find your way home and will surely need your money. There is no debt."

His blue eyes misted, and Bia feared he would cry.

"That is the way," Letty asserted. "If a person needs help, Daddy always said, you must give it, even if there is a cost."

Adrian smiled handsomely. "I will make it up to you ladies, I swear it."

"Oh, no need," Letty said. "Now we are friends."

He glanced at her, and Bia returned his gaze. The moment of contact lengthened. Woof panted happily.

"This is true," Bia agreed at last, hoping the cost would not be too high to pay.

****

Time passed easily in this manner. Quinn set out in the chaise for Ashford, to do the shopping. The hood down, Milton drove, and the chestnut horse pranced away in the melting snow.

Adrian watched them go. "Nice animal."

"The mare and chaise are ours," Letty informed him. "Milton thinks it very smart. Bia drove us up here from Dover."

"Did she?" he asked in surprise. He began to think Bianca Greenway capable of anything.

"Nothing wrong with women driving," Bia murmured, pulling at a stubborn knot in her thread.

"No, I suppose not. I just never knew any ladies who did so."

"The world is changing."

That much? he wondered. "But you were alone, with no protection?"

Bia plied her needle, forming intricate red flowers in the cloth. "We had a pistol."

Letty nodded. "Daddy taught us. Bia can shoot very well, and I am pretty fair. We would have had no compunction in shooting the ears off robbers."

Bia shook her head. "We traveled in broad daylight, Letty. No one troubled us."

Astounding. "Well, really. You ladies are impressive. But two lovely women alone on the road might have attracted fellows unconcerned with your money or your pistol."

"How confining," Letty cried. "Is it not so, Bia?"

"Definitely. Ladies should be as free as men to go where they like. Being wrapped in cotton wool is no way to live. An independent woman must not be bullied by goblins and outmoded rules."

"You have been away from England, Adrian," Letty added. "A lot has gone on. When did you go into the army?"

"Nearly five years ago." *What insanity*, he thought, but tried to make it seem sensible. "I was twenty, my education completed. I wanted to see the world, purchased my commission, and set out to do so."

"What did you see?" Bia asked.

The direct question overset him. Endless scenes of death and destruction, of misery and want, of mindless bravery, of loss and more loss, rose up before him. He had buried his youth in foreign mud. His courage had died five hundred times, and yet he had plodded on. There was no way back; he had to keep going. Frozen in the cold, baked in the sun, dirty, hungry, and desperately tired for months on end. His fine uniform bore the blood of thousands. His boots had walked in their souls. It had sickened him.

"Myself," he answered, "a fool, become a killer."

Her expression was forbearing. "You did what you had to. You fought for England and to survive. Forgive yourself, and go on."

He gazed at her. Bia's few words were an impossible comfort. And she meant it, had not made empty chatter. Letty rattled on, but Bia was deep, deep. When she spoke, she had considered what she said. Adrian wanted to sink into her arms and be redeemed.

Bia had seen sorrow cross his angelic face. He had endured, and many wounds did not show. A tremendous sympathy and tenderness for him surged up. In a tumult, unexpectedly, all the emotion Bia had walled up this last year burst forth and made her entire body tingle. She had to catch an extra breath and stuck her finger with the needle.

"Oh, blast."

Adrian laughed.

She sucked her fingertip.

"Bia swears," Letty confided. "I use the material. Give me a good ducal curse, Adrian."

"A euphemism?" he asked.

"Mercy! What is that?"

"A nicer word or phrase you can substitute for one deemed too blunt. Like over the hill, instead of old. Gone to their reward, instead of dead."

"No, I mean some jolly good insults."

"Read Shakespeare's plays. He is the master of the cutting remark." He grinned. "My uncle once called his neighbor a whoreson bug-eyed bastard. That was a good one."

The ladies gasped, astonished.

"Sorry. Uncle can be volatile if in a temper. Perhaps something milder? Bejabbers and the like? Zounds refers to God's wounds. Cripes stands for—"

Bia released her finger with a pop. "Enough!

Letty's mind is bent in the wrong direction as it is."

But Letty busily wrote it all down. Woof rolled over on his back toward the fire, his paws in the air. Adrian gazed at her.

"All I say is blast. Time to time."

"You are the epitome of a lady, Miss Bianca."

"Perhaps in Dover circles. I mean to expand my horizons."

"How so?"

She tilted her head. "Someday, I will go to London, buy beautiful gowns, hats, and slippers, and stride about town importantly. This will happen when Letty writes something brilliant and keeps me in luxury."

Letty declared, "You just wait, Bia. I will do it."

"I have every confidence, dear girl. We will try Bath, if all else fails."

"Why Bath?" Adrian asked.

"There are lots of visitors to study, and lectures, assemblies, and concerts that anyone may attend. I have a strong desire to leave Dover. We may be able to afford Bath when we sell our house. And we have this cottage to put on the market."

"Before the gully swallows it," Letty put in.

"We should have left here long ago," Bia explained, "but we dallied. The weather kept fine, and new surroundings were a relief. So we stayed. Quinn threatens to leave every day, but she stays, too."

"It is inertia," Letty said.

"That means resistance to change, Letty. I am pining for change."

Letty raised a finger. "It also means if you are in motion, you will stay in motion, or if still, you will remain so. Unless you are given a nudge either way.

We have remained quite still here, I must note."

Adrian found this remarkable. "I say, you ladies have been educated in the physical sciences?"

They both giggled.

"Well, you seem knowledgeable to me."

"We have common sense," Letty claimed.

"Which is better than no sense at all," Bia agreed. "Ah, here comes the chaise. Now we can have tea."

The girls went to aid the cook, and Adrian listened to their voices. Chatting with them took him back years, when he had amusing young ladies on his arm. Time had been infinite, when the world was new. Before everything else happened.

Much bustle in the kitchen, talk, the clink of dishware, and he caught what sounded like "Dewarr." He went on high alert. "Celebration…party." Adrian held his breath, but the talk ended.

Letty appeared, carrying a tray of cups and saucers. Bia followed with a teapot in a quilted cozy and a plate. The tray went on a nearby table.

"We have iced cakes," Letty announced. "These are in your honor, Adrian. We only get bread and butter for tea as a rule. Or muffins."

He remained outwardly tranquil and accepted a cup. When Bia passed the cake plate, he took one and promptly ate it. "Delicious. Did I hear something said about a celebration?"

"Some to-do in town. A Christmas party," Bia answered.

"Up at the castle," Letty added. "That is the home of the local despots, the Dewarrs."

"Townspeople call it a castle," her sister remarked, "but it must only be a big house. I am sure they are ordinary folks."

Letty shook her head. "Milton says they are bloodthirsty oppressors."

Bia sighed. "The fellow never heard of the term, Letty, but you have. I declare, your mind supplies facts where none exist. How will you be able to distinguish the truth? Curb your more fanciful impulses."

"Piffle. Actually, Milton used a much stronger term. I cleaned it up for your delicate ears."

Bia eyed her sister.

Adrian plotted how to get out of here and find out what was going on. For that, he needed to be able to stand up, at the least.

They had a horse and chaise, Adrian now knew and planned to steal them at the first opportunity. Or just the horse if he found a saddle. He could ride. He needed to get into town and put his ear to the ground. Satisfied with this outline, he accepted another cake.

****

The girls carried the tea things away and returned to find Adrian standing up. Bia took in his tall form, those endless legs, and his very gentlemanly presence. He stood straight despite his injuries, every inch the military man.

Letty rushed to aid him. "You will not fall?" she anxiously asked, taking his good arm. "You may be very weak and unsteady."

"I have to get up and try. See where I am."

Bia joined them but, having nowhere safe to put a helping hand, merely stood by. He shuffled his feet a little, took some steps, and padded around the room in stocking feet. Rather slowly, but upright. Adrian's positive expression and his courage touched her heart with a gentle flutter. *What a fine man he is.*

It is just his fascinating beauty, she told herself, and the unusual situation. *He came out of nowhere to show you how lonesome you are.* His story had impressed her. And the fact that, with a hole in his shoulder, here he was, on his feet, making a heroic effort to heal.

Once more about the room and Bia became so worried for him, she intruded on this hike. "Are you all right? Shall you sit down again?"

"One more circuit," he said, fatigue in his voice. When he came around again, Letty in attendance, Bia stood in his way.

"That is enough for now. You must not strain your wound."

He gazed down at her, his blue eyes warm. It made her giddy. Letty moved away. He reached out for Bia and put his arm around her shoulders. They took another step to the sofa, and blast him, he hugged her! A positive squeeze, this time. The flirt! Certain of it, she savored the daring adventure of his deliberate touch. Of his male strength.

Adrian sat down, appearing pleased. His generous mouth curved in a smile. "Made it. Thank you, ladies."

"You did very well," Letty praised.

"Yes, and what an able right arm," Bia pointedly remarked.

He grinned. "I am right-handed."

"Ah?"

His blue eyes sparkled. He knew what she meant.

"But I can do very well with my left," he added, "when required."

"No doubt."

Letty went to see if there were more cakes. Bia became a little wobbly to again be alone with him. Worried he would say something outlandish and hoping he might. She took a chair near him and picked up her embroidery.

"Beautiful Bianca," he whispered.

She took a stitch. "Folderol."

"If you had been on the dock, I never would have sailed."

"By that time, it would have been too late."

"At twenty years old," he scoffed, "nothing was too late."

Her work went in her lap. "I am nearly twenty. I hope it is not too late for me to find my life. As you did, joining the army."

"That was not my life goal, Bia, but an impulse of youthful hubris. The war is over for me, thank God. This is my life, today, here with you and Letty. And I am going home, to find what remains of my place there."

The talk made her wistful. "I have to make my future somehow, too. The days have blown away while I have been deciding. But I have not decided." She glanced aside. "Oh, I do not know what I mean to say."

"Perhaps your life will be made with another person," he suggested. "You will find him, and that will lead you on to other things."

Bia hopefully asked, "A fabled prince will seek me out?"

"Perhaps he already has," he remarked, his expression clever.

"Most convenient if he comes along of his free will. If I do not need to sojourn in Bath to find him."

"In the meantime, you have me," Adrian offered.

Her heart thumped irregularly. "Oh, do I?"

"Cast upon you by a twist of fate. And you saved my life, so I rather belong to you."

"Mercy, a bargain at the price."

"Yes, indeed. I show a little wear but am full of promise."

He was definitely flirting. Bia relished it. "Are you, sir? I should think many ladies await your return to Ashford. That is your home, you said?"

"Close by. No one waits, I assure you. No lady would, for nearly five years."

She disagreed. "They would wait. If they loved you."

He leaned toward her. "You would wait, would you not?"

"Yes, if my feelings were true."

"A very lucky man to find you, Bia."

"I vow he would be content. I would make sure of it. If I loved him."

His gaze became so fixed on her, it was as if he removed all her clothing. Without a qualm, Bia looked right back at him and, piece by piece, did the same.

****

Letty returned. "I had two more cakes. Quinn is cooking up a storm. She bought beefsteak and says you need meat to get well, Adrian."

"How kind of her."

"She had some trouble getting it because the butcher promised all his beef to the celebration at the castle."

Adrian paid strict attention. "Ah? What else did Quinn hear?"

She sat beside him. "Many aristocrats are coming, the grocer said."

"What day?"

"By Saturday, likely. Christmas Eve is on Sunday." Letty narrowly regarded him. "You must want to get home to your family for that."

Adrian, boxed in, could not lie. "Yes and no. It is complicated." He paused, regarding the sisters. "They think I am dead."

Bia glanced up from her sewing. "If that is so, who followed you and tried to shoot you?"

Tell them, he thought. "Someone may want my so-called demise to be true."

A silence fell, as they studied him. Damn, what to say? "My older brother, Dalton, was in charge of matters after our father died. One of the letters I received related…that my brother has also died." His indignation and anger swelled. "In a riding accident. This is preposterous! My brother was an excellent horseman. An extremely agile man, he never made physical mistakes of any kind. Never." He leaned forward earnestly. "I suspect dark dealings. The man who followed and shot me cannot have been acting on his own. Somehow, he knew I would come and waited for me."

"You were saved by the snowstorm!" Letty cried.

"Yes, and by you two ladies."

"Now they will think you dead again," Bia murmured, half to herself.

"Perhaps, since I have not walked in."

"Well, what are your plans, Adrian?" she inquired.

"To go into Ashford and speak to people who know me, if they still exist. Who can tell me further what has gone on, and who has been put in control of, uh, family affairs." He again shifted his position on the sofa. "The second letter I received," he irritably said, "contained a copy of a certificate saying that I had died honorably at Waterloo and where to apply for benefits."

Letty raised her hand and smothered a horrified laugh.

Bia, troubled, counseled, "You lack the strength as yet to ride to town."

"We could drive him," her sister quickly proposed. "In our company, no one would suspect it was Adrian. In case that fellow with the rifle is hanging about."

"No," he objected. "I cannot put you at risk."

"No one is after us, eh, Bia? It sounds an adventure to me. Think of the material!"

"You can afford to wait another day, Adrian," Bia advised.

"I have waited long enough."

"See how you feel in the morning, then."

Remarkable! "You would take me, Bia?"

"Yes, if you feel able."

"Tremendous," Letty said, clapping her hands. "Adrian can go in disguise, how about that?"

"Good idea," Bia agreed. "I wonder if there are more old clothes in this house? I will ask Quinn."

Adrian had to control his emotions. How tremendous of them. "You ladies have been uncommonly helpful to me. I will repay your every kindness, I swear."

"Skullduggery," Letty said, appreciating the word. "This beats the dueling mistresses."

Bia feared for him; Adrian saw it in her glance. Her concern delighted him. He would succeed in all this for her. And if he did, these two females would never journey to the wilds of Bath.

****

Adrian was helped to the kitchen and the best chair. Quinn gave him ample servings of beef, roasted potatoes, and carrots. Soft bread rolls and butter arrived, along with a bottle of red wine. This impressed Bia no end. Letty presented her glass expectantly.

"I am uncertain if you should have wine, Letty. It is not our habit."

"Pish-tosh. Let us make it our habit. It will have a cultivating influence."

"It builds blood," Quinn put in. "Good for himself."

"See there, Bia. One glass."

She reluctantly poured. Well, why not. She filled Adrian's glass and her own. They silently toasted.

Letty licked her lips. "Why, it tastes like fruit punch."

"Drink enough wine, and you will understand the term punch," Adrian instructed.

He attacked his plate, and Bia had a big drink. Oh, he could not cut the meat. With her clean knife and fork and as he smiled at her, she cut the beef into bites. Bia thought of poor James and her heart tensed, as if in fear of pain and loss.

Bia ate her food. Adrian would go away once he settled his affairs. She would take time in the new year to put this cottage on the market and leave here. As well, have done with the Dover property and see what came next. She would do whatever seemed sensible and, please, let it be something enjoyable. She longed for gaiety, extremely tired of drooping feelings and the dreary past. Of the endless war and emotions buried along with people. She had another drink of the wine, which made a pleasant glow in her middle.

"Quinn, Adrian needs a coat. Are there more old clothes in the house?"

Silence from Quinn at the sink.

"That might fit our guest?" Bia persisted.

"I ain't to talk of them, your grandmama said."

"That can hardly apply now," Letty offered. "Granny is moldering in the fens of Biddenden."

"I am uncertain if there are fens near Biddenden," Adrian thoughtfully remarked.

"No matter. Quagmires, then. These are good terms."

Bia got in a word. "Back to the clothes, Quinn. What is the secret there?"

Quinn energetically dried a pan, the towel flapping. "All right then. Your grandmama had a lover."

The two girls gasped in unison. Adrian chewed, his brows rising.

Quinn lifted her bosom righteously. "It is the honest truth, and I kept the secret all this time. But my work here is done. I be goin' to my auntie right soon and see no reason to keep my promise to folks gone over."

"Euphemism," Letty whispered.

Bia sliced more meat, and everyone had another helping. Adrian spooned up potatoes as Letty worked on the wine.

"Tell us," Bia asked.

Quinn strutted to the table. "Six years ago, it was. She sent him down here from her home in Biddenden and me with him. He suffered of a cough. She said the clean air would be good for him. And he were something, I can tell you. Big man, tall like this one, with a bush of black hair and such eyes as would drill holes in ye.

"He had a spry fellow that attended him. I kept the house, and your grandmama would come and visit every few days. In good weather, they would sit in the sun and hold hands. Or before the fire, talking and drinking tea. She bought him herbs and potions, but he coughed anyways. Not the consumption, something else had him in its grip."

"Did she sleep in his bed?" Letty asked.

"What a wicked, sinful girl you are!" Quinn chided.

Letty insisted, "Yes, but did she?"

"She loved him, so what account is it now?" the woman huffed. "He died, and the lady wept something sorrowful. Now she has passed, and I say let them be in peace."

"I totally agree, Quinn," Bia acknowledged, "and it was good of you to keep your word. We do not condemn Granny. She was a dear, loving woman."

"Granddad might have thought otherwise," Letty amended. "If he had still been around."

"Not for us to judge, Letty. Back to the clothing. Where is it?"

"Trunk upstairs, hall storeroom. I give some to Milton, but he be a shade careless for nice things. I meant to take 'em to the church bazaar after your grandmama went but did not get around to that."

"After this excellent meal, we will look for a coat," Adrian said and gave her one of his brilliant smiles.

Quinn beamed. "Mighty glad you do not cough,

Mister Adrian. Rice pudding for dessert."

"Cheers! I am a fortunate man." He tossed Woof a bite of meat, and the dog nimbly caught it.

Letty had another glass of wine and began to look dreamy around the eyes.

Bia was convinced in the last couple of days the planet had tipped sideways. Everything might slide to the edges, but she would hang on. Granny and a lover? Incredible.

They left the table, and Adrian tried the stairs on his own. Really, he was much better. Tomorrow would find him fit, and he would get his boots on. He paused at the top to rest, Bia right behind him. Letty followed along, yawning.

"Are you all right?" Bia asked him.

"Yes. Where is this storeroom?"

"At the end of the hall."

Bia took his good arm. How warm and gentle she was! They proceeded down the hallway, reached the door, and she opened it. Letty brought a lamp.

A few boxes lined the sides of the narrow room, along with several extra chairs. A leather trunk stood in the middle. Adrian sat on a wooden stool, as Bia opened the trunk and Letty held up the lamp. It was full of neatly folded clothing. Lavender bundles were on top, still fragrant. She sorted through several linen shirts, buckskin breeches, a tweed coat, a cloth sack of stockings and smalls, and at the bottom, a greatcoat.

"See here, Adrian," Bia said, shaking out the tweed coat. "This all looks suitable."

"It does," he agreed. "Now I can wash and change. I am feeling a little grubby."

"Grubby!" Letty laughed. "I am feeling very

sleepily. Seepy. Sleepy."

"Give me that lamp, Letty," Bia advised. "You are intoxicated."

"Am I?" She giggled.

"Go and lie down."

"I must note my reactions," the girl murmured and sauntered away, Woof right after her.

Adrian chose a shirt and a pair of the buckskins. She took the cloth bag, coat, and the greatcoat, and they left the room, Bia holding the lamp high. She draped the coats over the banister, left the lamp on the table, and they started down.

"I am sure you wish to bathe," she said. "We must make do for you, with no one to attend you. I could ask Milton in the morning."

"I will not attempt a full bath," he assured her. "I am accustomed to washing, if at all, in whatever I had. A bath can wait."

"Would you like to wash up a little now, Adrian?"

"Yes, if I may."

They strolled to the kitchen, now empty.

"Quinn has retired to her room on this floor."

Adrian admired her movements as Bia put the kettle back on the stove and found a large pan. She located a bar of soap in a flowered pottery bowl, a flannel, and a towel. The lamplight shone on her pretty hair and the curve of her cheek. A wave of desire arced through him. So fair and young, so vulnerable, and sweetly female. How long had it been since he touched a woman? Years, a lifetime.

He unbuttoned the flannel shirt. Freed his good arm and labored to raise the other. Without a word, she helped him take it off.

"Good. Your bandage is clean. Oh, Adrian, you cannot manage. Your shoulder is too sore."

He did not answer.

"And you are very tired."

She was convincing herself, he knew, and waited. Bia hesitated, then turned to the stove and poured the warmed water into the bowl. She passed the flannel over the soap and handed it to him. He did his best, rinsed that off, and she patted his face and neck dry. Adrian thought he might break into tears.

"Bia," he began.

"It is all right. I know I am most uncomfortable if I do not wash."

She proceeded to move hastily over his chest and good arm. Squeezed out the cloth and washed his back and the other arm, her touch tender. With fresh water she sponged off the soap. Then she washed over him again, and he felt clean. Adrian rubbed his jaw.

"I need to shave. A razor is in my bag."

"Do you want it?"

"Yes, please."

Bia handed him the towel and left. What a delightful female, as charming and desirable as any he had ever met. Maybe even more so.

****

Bia went to the sitting room, put the bag on the sofa, and unbuckled it. Pushed aside articles of clothing, found a book tied with a cord, and a black leather box. She snapped it open to find a folded razor and closed it again. Below that lay a brown packet under two mud-stained letters. The top one was addressed to Captain the Honorable Adrian Blackmere Dewarr, 2nd Coldstream Regiment, Headquarters,

Brussels, Belgium. HOLD FOR DELIVERY.

Bia read it again, dropped the bag, clutched the razor, and marched back to the kitchen. There he stood in all his blond glory, bare from the waist up.

"You scoundrel," she hotly stated. "What is your game? You have some sort of intrigue going with the local despots? Skulking around here with folks shooting at you and no wonder! Who are you, really? An imposter? A spy?"

"Eh?"

She slammed down the razor box. "I saw a letter, addressed to Captain the Honorable Dewarr. Is that you, or did you steal it? Have you come to fool them like you fooled us?"

"Oh, hell," he moaned.

"I should say! And us waiting on you hand and foot, while you could have gone up there and done whatever you came for."

"I was on my way to do just that, when shot and unhorsed. I am Adrian Dewarr, yes, and—"

She angrily cried, "You could have said!"

He stood straight, his expression defensive. "If I had, you would not have treated me the same."

She shook her head and dumped the water into the sink.

"Would you have?" he demanded. "No, things always change when I say who I am."

"Insanity." Bia touched the kettle. "I do not care who you are. The water is still warm, so shave." She opened a drawer. "Here is tooth powder and an extra brush. Clean yourself up, and tomorrow you are out, do you hear? We will drive you into Ashford, then it is goodbye."

"You want me to be killed?" he objected grimly.

"If you deserve it." She turned to leave him.

He reached out his enormous arm and blocked her way. "Bianca, let me explain."

She stepped away from him.

"I am who I said. I just feared to tell you my last name. You spoke of a pistol; maybe you would like to shoot me, too. Now I know you would not. I intended to tell all tomorrow, when we went into town. Where I hope I can find out who has taken my place, because somebody has! And they want me dead for certain, as they had hoped." Damn it all! He had to tell her. "The fact is, Bia, I suspect my brother was murdered."

In one stride, he stood next to her. She gazed up at him with wary green eyes. "Do not run away from me, Bia. You are the grandest woman I have ever met. I treasure our acquaintance."

"You are just needy."

"You have no idea how needy. Being around you for these two days has been electrifying. Your beauty and graciousness, your willingness to help a stranger. Your easy, friendly ways. After all I have been through, I had about lost faith in everything. Then there you were. An angel, come to save me, to give me hope again, to make me remember how much…I have had to hold myself back. Just to put my hands on you would be a joy."

Her lovely face. Did she believe him, could she trust him? He put his arm around her. "I have to say, Bia. I want so much to kiss and hold you."

Both her hands went to his chest. "No."

"I knew you would refuse me, and it broke my heart."

She gave him a push. "Stop this."

"How about one small kiss? After I use the tooth powder."

The girl laughed merrily. "Is this how you do it, you rascal? How you get your way? By being amusing and telling more stories than Letty?"

"I stand here before you, honest as the sun."

She slipped away from his arm. "Which might scorch me. Come along. Finish up here."

"I will shave tomorrow." He took the powder and brush, went to the sink, and cleaned his teeth. Bia hung up the towel and flannel and tidied the table. What a sweetheart, Adrian mused, with a trim figure and lush breasts. He breathed her fragrance and smelled her lovely hair. He rinsed the pan at the pump. Clean as possible, now he would take that kiss.

Chapter Four

Adrian turned to her with great deliberation. Bia, unafraid, raised her chin defiantly and held out his shirt. He put it on the chair.

"Are you not cold?" she asked.

His warm hand clasped her waist. She had not the slightest impulse to get away as he bent toward her.

"I wanted to feel you against my skin."

Bia shivered all over as he put his face into her hair.

"And smell you. Feel your weight."

He nuzzled her ear, and her breath halted.

"You are all woman, kind, gentle, and loving. Any man would value you. So I should like to have you for my own."

He is a cunning rake! Who else would have such practiced talk? "Are these reckless words, sir? I am unaccustomed." She pushed at her hair. "Perhaps in your elevated circles—"

"Stop right there!" he ordered. "I told you things would change, so do not let them."

She gazed up at him.

"I want it to stay as we were, Bia, friends together."

"I meant to tease."

"Oh, did you?"

And Adrian kissed her lips. Warm, enticing,

overwhelming, desirable, forbidden, enlightening. Every emotion wove into twisting strands of love and fear, risk and desire. The impulse arose to take every gamble, jump into the air even if she fell, gravity gone, caution forgotten. His tongue traced the seam of her lips, searching. In disbelief, she opened her mouth to protest, and he invaded her being.

Bia, bewildered, went limp, but Adrian kept her upright. The kiss deepened. She put her arm around his neck, her hand on his stubbly cheek, kissed him back by sheer instinct, and let it all happen. This encouraged him, and in moments the kitchen was an inferno.

His hand roamed all over her back and caressed her bottom. She bit his good shoulder and tugged at a handful of his silky hair. He pulled her closer, and she felt all of him, including the solid place in his trousers. She slowly climbed back up to the surface of reality.

"Bianca, you are most desirable," he whispered.

"I should go," she breathed.

"I would give a fortune to make love with you."

Bia searched over his amazing face, trying to really see him. "I will settle for the two pounds, if you will kiss me once more."

He did. And she did. Dreams and fiery longings knitted around her until she fought for breath.

"Bia," he said, his voice husky. "I have waited to find you."

"Mmmm."

"So do not think ill of me."

Bia smiled and confessed, "I wanted to kiss you, to feel like that. Although…"

"What?"

"I did not know how much. So," she decisively

said, "we must have a sleep. Come. To the stairs." Bia took his arm, he caught up the shirt, and they slowly walked that direction.

Tomorrow he will have forgotten all this madness, Bia consoled herself, and maybe she would too.

****

Thursday

Once again, Bia woke to the sagging mattress. Letty snuggled under the comforter with her, Woof content to lie between them on the top, his head on his paws.

"Letty," she mumbled. "When do you sleep?"

The girl leaned on her elbow. "Scant time for that, sister. Think of all I would miss. For instance, dalliances in our very own kitchen."

She rubbed her eyes. "Ha. Milton and Quinn in a heated embrace?"

"Nay. You and the gallant captain."

Bia sat up, jostling the dog, and pulled the comforter from her sister. "You snoop and eavesdropper!"

Letty tugged it back. "Well, my stomach ached, so I came down to get a drink of milk. And there you two were, and you were washing him! What a picture. I could not turn away from such material, so I sat on the steps and listened. Then it all got better."

"Traitorous, treacherous girl," Bia complained, bashing her sister with a pillow. "Is everything grist for your mill?"

"He kissed you, and it sounded like you did not object." Letty gazed into the middle distance. "Now we know he, too, may be a tyrant and autocrat from the castle."

"He is just a cousin or some such."

"Captain the Honorable?"

"We do not know what that means in the British Army. Today, as you likely heard, you nosy-box, we shall journey into Ashford and find out. I will go for water, and we can have a wash before he wakes."

Letty jumped up and hurried away, Woof on her heels. Bia got out of bed, pulled on her robe, and padded downstairs.

Quinn, somewhat bleary-eyed, sat at the table with her dish of coffee. "What hours you folk be keepin', the sun hardly up."

"I came for hot water." She poured from the kettle to the ewer and added water at the pump, then hefted it, staggered out and up the stairs. Bia trotted along to Letty's room, a litter of papers and books, and gave her half.

"I should like a bath in the nice, warm kitchen." Letty sighed, pulling her robe closer.

"When we have some privacy again. Meantime, do what you must."

Bia went along to her room. Poured water into the bowl and washed enough to satisfy. Unbraided and brushed out her long hair and fastened it into a chignon at the back of her neck. Donned her best gown, a blue-green light wool with long sleeves and embroidered flowers along the modest neckline. Added her good brown half boots and was ready.

She strolled out, hopeful for the day, and listened at Adrian's door. Small noises made her heart bump. She tapped.

"Come." His deep voice jarred her brain. She peeped in.

"Bia, just in time. Come in, come in. I have done everything else but cannot get these buckskins on. They require two hands."

Bia stepped inside. There he sat, the breeches to his knees. "Oh. Um, are they too tight?"

"No, it's just…" He frowned. "I cannot manage with only one good hand and arm."

She had the mad impulse to laugh, he was so vexed. "Can you stand?"

"Yes."

"All right then. Do that, if you will, and I will pull them up."

He stood, and Bia went to the back of him, so as not to look at his…She tugged, her face near his bottom. This was worse. She moved back to the front and tugged some more. He put his hands on her shoulders, leaned down, and nuzzled her neck. She laughed. He laughed.

Letty bowled in the door. "Saints above. Before breakfast?"

Woof panted with extra vigor, wagging his tail.

"Come and help. Better still, go downstairs and find Adrian's boots."

She raced away, the dog's claws clicking on the floor.

"Now, Adrian," Bia directed. "Behave yourself, or we will never get these on."

"Yes, ma'am. Take that side, and I will get this one."

Together, they managed to clothe him. He buttoned the falls, Bia tucked in one side of his shirt, and he got the other. The buckskins were a little loose at the waist but would do.

He grinned handsomely. "What a team we make, pretty Bia."

"You need a valet."

"And what do you need?" he murmured, stepping closer.

"Breakfast."

Letty rushed back with the boots.

Getting him into these proved easy. They were old, soft leather and, with a little assistance, went right on. Adrian stood, steadier on his feet than he had been.

"Thank you, ladies, thank you. Now, this is much better, eh?"

"They make you taller," Letty remarked. "How fine you must have been in your captain's uniform."

He gazed directly at her. "Ah ha. I thought I heard you on the stairs last night. You may care to know, Miss Letty, that I can hear you at a hundred paces. It has kept me alive."

Letty, chastised, asked, "Are you angry?"

"No, I admire your resourcefulness, clever girl. Look you, I can use my arm some." He lifted his stiff arm from the elbow and, with one finger, touched his nose, making the girls laugh. "Shall we go have breakfast?"

Woof ran ahead, and the three left the room. The ladies gently supporting him, they made it to the stairs and started down.

In the kitchen, Bia was glad to find Quinn in good form, applying herself to brewing more coffee. Tasty food smells filled the room.

"And good day to you, sir," the woman greeted Adrian, looking him up and down. "You seem to have growed."

"It is the boots, ma'am."

"Sit down, all of you."

Coffee poured, a platter of coddled eggs and sautéed ham offered, everyone had a serving, and they began to eat. A plate of currant muffins arrived, with butter and jam. Bia found it prudent to take a muffin before Letty and Adrian ate them all.

How fine he seemed this morning, so much healthier. His beard was golden, like his hair. Bless Doctor Fox and his malodorous paste, they had done the job. Of course, he must still take care. They would watch out for him. Bia did not think of his tremendous kisses or the way his body had felt against hers. Hardly at all, just now and then. She wished she could press the memory like a flower, so it would not fade.

Quinn poured more coffee, and they drank.

"How stand we for our journey into town?" he asked.

"We are ready, eh, Bia?" Letty inquired.

"Yes, if you feel up to it, Adrian."

"I do."

They stood. Adrian bowed slightly in Quinn's direction. "Ma'am, a top-notch breakfast and a champion muffin."

The cook flushed and murmured the tiniest of thanks. The three headed to the stairs.

"One thing," Bia said. "If we wish to disguise you, we need a hat to cover your hair."

"Right," he agreed. "That would be a tipoff."

Letty piped up. "Adrian can wear my blue hat. That is stretchy."

"Worth a try, Letty. Then with the coat and everything, no one should notice us. That is, no one cares if we come and go, but you must be a little hidden."

"He can stoop over and appear dotty," Letty suggested. "That is a euphemism for elderly."

At the landing, Adrian bent low and hobbled along, dragging one boot. She and Letty went into gales of laughter.

At last, the lot of them emerged in the hall. Bia, in her warm, dark blue pelisse, took in Adrian's remarkable appearance. The gray greatcoat had capes and made him appear menacing, but it fit. Letty handed him the blue hat, and he covered his pretty hair. Bia tucked in a few strands. The snug wool cap made his eyes bluer.

"You forgot to shave."

"Do you mind?" he whispered.

"No." She fussed over him, until Letty gave her a poke.

"Let us go! We still have to find Milton and get him to hitch the horse."

Down the stairs again and out the back door. Milton stood in the yard, considering the day.

"Ho, Milton," Bia called, "we need the chaise."

"Do you, now?" he muttered, puffing on his pipe.

"We have important business in Ashford," Letty informed him.

Milton turned. "Bringin' the frozen feller, are ye?"

Bia impatiently gestured. "Here he is, Milton, standing upright."

"Too many of yuz to fit."

This man! "We will make do."

"Allow me to assist you," Adrian said, stepping forward. "I have a bad arm, but I can help."

Milton released a great quantity of smoke. "No, sir, I be doin' it. Just you wait right there, will not take a moment!" He scurried away to the barn, a structure large enough to hold a horse, the chaise, and Milton.

"What got him moving?" Letty inquired.

She shrugged. "Adrian acted so gentlemanly, Milton was embarrassed."

"No," he replied, "I was just courteous. He worried I would pull rank and give orders. Many soldiers expressed such an attitude toward officers. But if you were fair, they came around."

Bia filled with admiration for Adrian. What a fine captain he must have been. She thought over his details of the battle at Hougoumont Chateau and how famous that engagement had become. Napoleon himself, in a pique at the standoff, had ordered the farmhouse continuously shelled until the whole structure caught fire and burned. Where Adrian had been at that moment, even he did not know. If he had died there…She repressed the thought.

Milton led out the prancing chestnut, harnessed to the chaise. Woof, anticipating a trip, ran in circles.

"Here ye be, sir," he said, handing the reins to Adrian. "Ready to trot."

"Well done. Thank you, Milton."

They were given one of Milton's toothy grins. "The mare be an easy go. Take good care." He walked toward the house, leaving a trail of pipe smoke that smelled of burnt oranges.

Adrian glanced over the chaise. A fit enough vehicle, but small. "Must I ride on the running board?" he asked.

"No. Woof rides there."

"Yes," Bia affirmed. "He has the vapors if we try to leave him behind."

"He fears being abandoned again," Letty sagely said. "Watch." The dog, as always, waited at her feet. "Stay, Woof."

The dog's expression turned doleful, he hung his head, then he fell right over on his side like he was dead.

"Stop, Letty," Bia said, "it is too mean."

Letty bent down. "All right, Woof, honey lamb, you can come for a ride."

The dog bounded up, full of life.

"Go and get in your basket."

The dog loped to the back of the chaise and climbed into a deep basket fastened to the running board, panting happily.

"Now then," Bia said. "I believe we can all fit."

"You can sit on my lap, Bia," he offered.

"You first," she answered, hiding her smile.

Adrian climbed in, scooted over, then Letty, then Bia. He had not reckoned how small the two of them were. A pair of little girls had held his life in their hands. Yet Bia was every desirable woman that had ever lived, all in one being. These two were extraordinary. He had never known such.

"Give the horse a tap with the whip, Adrian," Letty advised.

He took the reins. "Sit back, Miss Letty, and I will show you how it is done." He made kissing noises, and the horse pulled them forward. With his good arm and hand, he guided the vehicle around the house, up to the road, and turned toward Ashford. By God, he was on his way and soon would find out the truth.

They bounded along the narrow track, past sleeping orchards and fallow fields. They passed a few scattered houses. A flock of sheep moved across a meadow patchy with snow. Stands of poplars and thin pine woods lined the verges. Woodsmoke hung on the air. Cottages appeared, then buildings of all sizes and shapes. The town had grown since he had last been here.

He had quarreled with Dalton about the army. He had no cause to go to war, did not have to go, he was needed at home. What as, Adrian had thought, your subordinate, your representative? Jesus, he had been stupidly proud, too stubborn, too big a fool, and now his brother was gone.

Abruptly they reached the crossroad, turned right, and entered the High Street. Adrian glanced around at shoppers and strollers but saw no one hostile. He drove on. Reaching the end of the second block, he came to the neat, whitewashed house he sought.

No one nearby, he turned to his friends. "This is the home of Doctor Knowles, that Fox mentioned. He tended Dalton and me since we were infants. I know I can trust him."

"What can we do to help?" Bia asked.

"Come with me."

"Right!" exclaimed Letty, trying to get out first.

"Violetta, you monkey, wait a minute." Bia climbed down, and Letty tumbled out. Immediately, they were joined by the dog. Adrian got out, dropped the harness weight, bent way over, and gathered the coat around him.

"Help me along here, lazy gels. Help me along!" he cackled. They assisted him up the walk to the door. The dog leapt up the steps, full of curiosity. Adrian glanced around, saw no one, and twisted the brass bell.

The door was promptly answered by a woman in a white apron, likely a housekeeper.

"Good day," Adrian said. "We wish to see the doctor, please."

"Doctor's not in," she asserted, "permanent like. You must go and see Doctor Fox, just down the street."

"Tell him Adrian Dewarr has come to call."

"No, I am saying to you—"

"Stand aside, Martha." An older man came forward and stared at Adrian. "It is you! Adrian, my lad, whatever, how? Come in, come in."

They all stepped into the wide foyer, even the dog, who politely sat down. The doctor, a ruddy man with thinning ginger hair and a cheery appearance, reached to embrace him, but Adrian held the man off.

"Fresh bullet wound through the left shoulder, healing nicely. Doctor Fox's work."

The doctor gestured. "Come into the study. Martha, bring tea."

"What about this dog?" the woman inquired.

"Dogs do not drink tea." The man led them to a comfortable, spacious room, and they took chairs. He beamed at Adrian. "Tell me all."

"First allow me to introduce my friends, Miss Bianca Greenway and Miss Violetta Greenway. These ladies saved my life when I was ambushed, unhorsed, fell, and hit my head. The nearly spent bullet probably passed through me to down my mount."

"Ladies, welcome to you. Who did the deed, Adrian?"

"I am unsure but have suspicions."

The gentleman registered sorrow. "I was informed Dalton had been killed."

"What were the details, sir? I only lately found out. It was a shock."

"And a hideous farce, in my opinion. Occurred tenth October, somewhere up in the castle wood, hunting. Low branch hit him, it was said, and broke his neck."

"Dalton would never have made such an error," Adrian cried, "even at full gallop! And he knew the woods like the palm of his own hand."

"It raised a storm, Adrian, I can tell you. No one could credit it."

Jesus, how horrible. "Was he alone?"

"No, your cousin Walter and several others were with him."

Adrian grumbled, "Walter! That leech!"

"Constable Fugate could not get a straight story but had no proof anything had been amiss. Tenants and workers on the place came into town and petitioned for an investigation, but nothing could be done without other witnesses."

"Where was my uncle in all of this?"

"In Vienna, helping to draw up peace treaties. I wrote and last heard he is on his way home. You know he loved Dalton."

"Everyone loved Dalton," Adrian mournfully said. "Everyone."

A maid served tea. Woof gazed up at her face, then at the tray. Again, he politely sat down, thumping his tail.

"Miss Greenway, would you pour out?" the doctor inquired. "So fine to have such pretty women in this room. Adrian knows how to pick them. Have a shortbread, little lady?"

"Thank you, sir," Letty replied, taking one, as Bia poured. "We are aiming to save Adrian from murderers. Suggest a plan."

The doctor laughed, jiggling his belly. "I say mount a siege, before the evil ones descend."

"What do you mean?" Adrian asked, accepting a cup.

"Obviously, it has been determined enough mourning has been done. The new order is set to arrive on the Saturday, I believe, Walter at the head of the phalanx. Adrian, everyone thought that you died at Waterloo. With Dalton gone, he means to insert himself and celebrate the holiday at the castle."

The whole tangle made him livid, his brother cruelly taken, the ambush, the sneak Walter at the heart of it all. His blood would boil and foam over. "Well, I did not die! I was shot, stabbed, suffered a concussion, lost my memory, sweated with fever, and nearly starved to death, but here the bloody hell I am. Pardon my anger, ladies. Followed from Dover and shot in the dark, in a snowstorm, to be sure I would not show up and trouble anyone. You tell me if this is not a giant scheme to take everything in a stinking coup." He drank his tea and smoldered.

Bia spoke, her voice soft. "You say, Doctor, that no one of importance has yet arrived up at the, ah, castle?"

"No, Miss Greenway. Staff are handling preparations, Martha has informed me. Draining the markets of foodstuffs. The plan, I heard, is to come the six miles from Walter's home at Charing Saturday around noon in a caravan. Folks are being encouraged to line the High Street to welcome the party."

Adrian found this to be disgusting pomp, and his fury grew. He would kill them all.

"Then, perhaps," Bia quietly said, "Adrian can be at the castle waiting to welcome them as well. That will make a nice holiday surprise, will it not?"

"And knock a hole in somebody's arrangement," Letty joyfully agreed.

Adrian suddenly saw how simple it could be. How properly, graciously poisonous. That sneak and parasite Walter would get more than a public comeuppance. He would hang.

****

Bia labored to digest all this information, uncertain exactly what had been discussed. The place they referred to as a castle must be a large farm property. Their home in Dover was called Prosper Manor for unknown reasons but was only an everyday house. Whatever it consisted of, the land or house was of great importance to Adrian, so he was determined not to lose it. His poor brother possibly done in, and now he was at risk? She spoke again.

"To avoid any unpleasantness, perhaps we could call upon this Constable Fugate for aid? His presence might ensure that no one loses their temper."

The doctor chuckled. "A wise young lady, Adrian."

Adrian smiled, his expression affectionate. "Absolutely, and a most valuable ally, along with her sister. I fell into good fortune."

"He almost fell into a deep gully when he was hurt, but we saved him," Letty related.

"They did, or I would not be sitting here. It seems to me, Doctor, that the next thing to do is go up to the castle and make my presence known."

"I agree. Set the stage, eh? While you do that, I will step over to the constable's office, speak to Fugate, and tell him what we think. Because I agree, Adrian. Dalton was cruelly murdered."

"I have little doubt of it."

"We can linger in town," Letty suggested. "If we would be in the way."

"Yes," Bia encouraged, "please take the chaise and we will wait."

Adrian regarded them. "I cannot lose you. You must come, too. What say you?"

"Hoorah!" said Letty.

"Will you go with me, Bia?" Adrian asked in a low voice. "Then you will know what I am about, what it means to me. What I have to do."

Still uncertain, she whispered, "Yes, I will."

"Thank you." He turned back to the doctor. "Doctor Knowles, you have been of great help. I understand everything better than I did."

Everyone stood. The men shook hands.

"I am at your service, Adrian," the doctor said with vigor. "An old fellow now, but I yet have some force. We shall see this out."

"I will speak with you next, sir, up at the castle?"

"Until then. So fine to meet you, ladies," the gentleman gallantly said.

The girls curtsied, and Adrian put on his snug hat. As they left the house, he again assumed the stance of an old man, Woof loping along. They made it to the chaise, and Bia lifted the harness weight so as not to break his disguise. They resumed their places, each very watchful. The mare took them back up the High

Street and out of the town center.

Adrian worried as he drove. He had not told Bia everything, anxious nothing should change in their relationship. All kinds of questions may intrude when she knew more. She might back away from him. He would lose the easy friendship, the talk, those hot kisses. He did not want to let her go. Now he had perhaps waited too long to speak and reveal himself.

Both females had gone quiet. He tried to stir up conversation. "Chances are we can have a good lunch when we arrive."

"Something other than ham would be appreciated," Letty remarked.

"What do you grow there?" Bia asked. "On your farm?"

"Grow? Oh, uh, when last home, various grains, hay, and a good deal of produce. Some varieties we cultivate in a glasshouse, or we did. Apple and pear trees in the orchard." He gazed out over the land. "A long time to be gone, five years."

"Then you will be glad to be home," she said.

A rain of emotions invisibly pummeled his chest, pushing his breath away. "Yes. Yes, I will."

They entered the lane leading up to the hilltop, the mare pulling. Crested it, and the view hit him with a mixture of sweet sadness and deep joy. He turned to the women. "There it is. Marlowe Castle."

Letty stood up, rocking the chaise.

Bia stared, unable to believe her eyes. Down a long gravel drive stood, if not a blasted castle, a mansion of considerable proportions. Blocky stones in a range of tan-grays formed a long façade, then grew into double towers rising up four stories, with crenellations on the tops. Dormant formal garden beds and evergreens ornamented the foundations. Wings angled off to the sides. Other outbuildings ranged around the property, including a long stable block, where horses grazed in a penned area. Farther along were a large number of cows. Fields stretched beyond. She was struck dumb, then she became hotly angry.

Letty petulantly sat down. "Well, I guess you think you are pretty shrewd, Adrian."

Bia joined in. "Of all the crust! Pretending to be a returning soldier. Just an ordinary fellow with a farm and mean relations. You must have had a good laugh fooling two peasants."

"I am not a peasant," Letty objected. "Just get out of our chaise and take yourself down there to your fiefdom or whatever you call it."

"And you owe us two pounds," Bia thundered. "You can send a lackey with it. But be quick, because we are leaving."

"Yes, indeed," Letty seconded. "We are going to Bath where gentlemen tell the truth."

"And do not carry on elaborate charades." Tears stung her eyes, how could he?

"So take a walk," Letty commanded.

Bia had an attack of conscience. "No, the beggar is hurt. We will drive him down there to his—Give me the reins."

Letty snatched them from his hand.

"Do I have nothing to say about this?" Adrian demanded.

"No!" the girls shouted as one.

What could Bia do? She was most reluctant. This had all evolved into something else. She sensed a threat, that the episode had turned against her favor. His family…Oh, she did not know. His uncle in Vienna, arranging peace treaties? Doubt sat on her shoulders. This had all been such a mad affair.

Bia snapped the reins, her thoughts in a tumult, and the mare gamboled down the hill. The things he had said, the way he had looked at her, those cunning hugs! Nuzzling her ears, making her go all mushy. Just a rakehell and scoundrel after all. Toying with them, playacting, eating their muffins. When they told Quinn, she would have kittens.

And she had fallen for all of it. Shame and disgrace swept over her. She had put on his clothes! If word of this ever reached anywhere civilized, she would be ruined forever, and Letty with her. They would be old maids. In Bath. A tear slipped down her cheek, and she brushed it away.

Bia guided the horse around a circular approach to a wide granite porch and a carved door big enough to admit a giant.

"What exactly is this?" Letty asked him, her tone unfriendly.

"The principal residence of the Earls of Marlowe."

"Ohhhhh," Bia groaned. "Just get out."

Adrian stepped down. "Damn it, Bia, this is completely unfair," he protested. "I told you things would change. All I had to do was show you the property, and right away all your prejudices slipped into place."

"Horsefeathers," Letty murmured.

"It is true," he asserted. "If I had been heir to a blacksmith, would you have made all this fuss? No! But let me be somebody other, and off you go, counting up my failures. Because I never measure up to the common idea of who I should be!" he yelled. "I am just a man, and this is my house, and so there."

All this commotion attracted a dignified butler who now appeared at the massive door. "I must object," he began.

Adrian turned and took off the blue hat, exposing his sunny hair. "Hello, Rodgers. How are you?"

The stout older man, all in black, his white shirt crisp, supported himself on the doorjamb. "Adrian!" he murmured. "Praise God." Then he smiled widely and bowed. "Lord Marlowe. Welcome home at last."

"My thanks. I have guests." He held out his hand to Bia. "Will you not come in, just for a little while?"

Lord Marlowe, was it? The immense nerve! The butler's eyes were on her, and Adrian's glance so hopeful, her heart trembled. "Just for a minute."

Bia took his hand, and he helped her down, the contact subdued by her gloves. Letty jumped out the other side, to be joined by Woof, his tail wagging furiously. She threw the quilted blanket over the horse, and they climbed the steps. The smiling butler held the door wide and took no notice of the dog. Bia reluctantly gave up her pelisse. Letty handed him her spencer.

"We never thought to see you again, sir," the man softly said. "The staff will rejoice. Oh, my lord, there is much to relate. We have been turned upside to. And there are constant intruders, folk who, by rights, should not be here."

Adrian placed his hand on the man's arm. "Steady on, Rodgers. There will be no more intrusions or foul deeds. I am back, and we will figure this out."

"Oh, sir, what they did," he grieved.

"I begin to know. Step down to the kitchens, if you will, and see to lunch for three."

"We cannot stay," Bia quickly said.

"Yes, you can. Whatever is available, Rodgers."

"Yes, my lord." The butler hurried down the hall.

"Come this way, my friends," Adrian coaxed.

Letty could scarcely follow him fast enough. Bia lagged behind but wanted to see where he went.

Adrian strode through double doors and into a vast drawing room filled with light from tall windows. There were beautiful rugs, paintings, and art pieces. Handsome furnishings, gay colors, and an air of ease and plenty prevailed. A fire crackled in a huge stone fireplace. It all made her head hurt.

Woof stretched out before the blaze. Letty studied a small carving of a reclining nude man, circling the table to see all sides.

Everything had spun out of Bia's control.

"Will you not sit down?" Adrian entreated. "I know all this has been a surprise, and truly, I did not mean to deceive you. But if someone has the temerity to shoot me, I need time to decide who did it and why. And you two marvelous ladies took me in with such generosity and loving kindness that I—"

Bia raised her hand. "You acted your part, Captain. Just stop with all the tra-la. You did what you did, and we did what we did, so let us hear no more of it."

"We can stay for a short time, Bia," Letty announced. "May I ask, is this carving old?"

"About two hundred years," Adrian answered.

"Splendid. While you talk Bia around, might I see the library?"

He pointed. "Through those pocket doors."

"Come, Woof." Off she went, the dog following.

"Do not keep standing there, Bia. Let us sit down."

She sat on a plushy, wine velvet settee. He crowded in next to her.

"I will straighten all this out," he insisted. "You have heard details of the problem. Thinking me dead, my uncle out of the country, they did for my brother and thought no one would be the wiser. Then somehow, they found out I was alive and on my way home and tried to pop me, too. But I am on my own ground now. Death was hurled at me by experts, Bia, and my murderous cousin is no match for what I faced. Not him or his henchmen."

She listened, noting the change in his attitude. He was harder, angrier, more determined. Stronger, more forceful. It was all impossible, and Bia longed to leave and never think of him again.

"I see you are worried for me," he murmured.

"I am not," she denied.

"Yes, you are. You care for me, Bia. We have grown close in these hectic days. You saved my life and I sincerely believe I am falling—"

A carriage rattled up to the house. Adrian stood, his whole stance ready for trouble. Then he started. "God above! It is my uncle!" He hastened to the doors.

Bia stood up and peeped out the front windows. A man in a flowing cape and tall hat descended from a splendid carriage and stepped to the porch. Adrian greeted him with open affection.

Oh, dear. They had stayed too long. Where had Letty gone to?

Chapter Five

Adrian jubilantly greeted his beloved uncle. He explained about his shoulder as Rodgers took his hat and cape. "Ambushed on the way here and rescued by a pair of angels. Come and meet them. How was the crossing?"

"Very good. I traveled on the *Tempest*, luckily headed this way."

"Make that four for lunch, Rodgers."

"Yes, my lord."

"Adrian, tell me all. We thought you lost at Waterloo," Uncle marveled, as they entered the drawing room. "What happened?"

"Wounded at the siege of Hougoumont Chateau, then invalided to Brussels. They crossed me off the lists when the place burned to the ground. I lost my wits for a time, but they patched me up and here I am, some the worse for wear."

Bia huddled near the window.

"Ah," he exclaimed, reaching her, "one of my rescuers. Allow me to present Miss Bianca Greenway. My uncle, Lawrence Gatewood Dewarr, Duke of Hayworth."

Bia curtsied deeply, giving Adrian an acid look. "Your Grace."

Letty returned with Woof, and both gazed up at his uncle.

"Here is the other, Miss Violetta Greenway, Bia's younger sister, who is a writer."

Letty sank in a half curtsey, her luminous green eyes taking him in. "Indeed, I am, Your Grace. Call me Letty. I must warn you, I constantly seek fresh material."

"Lucky for you, Miss Letty, I know secrets. I am honored, ladies. I am thrilled, my lad, that you are safe home. For God's sake, let us all sit down. Adrian, brandy."

Adrian went to a table with decanters and poured two glasses, not wanting his uncle to drink alone. Gave one glass to him and sat down by Bia, who leaned away.

"And what manner of dog is this?" Uncle Lawrence asked, rubbing Woof's shaggy ears.

"Silent," Letty offered. "He does not bark."

"Fortuitous."

"Not for him, but he is happy enough."

Uncle's attention moved to Bia. Adrian sipped the brandy.

"How did you rescue my wayward nephew?"

"By chance, Your Grace. We found him in the snow, shot, unconscious, his horse dead. We took him into the house, hoping he would live."

"It was more than that," Adrian promptly said. "They took excellent care, paid for the doctor, ladled food into me, and helped me hobble around. It was wonderful of them, or I would have died for sure, pleasing my enemies."

"My word," Uncle breathed.

Adrian nodded. "All true, sir, bizarre as it sounds."

"Then," Bia declared, her green eyes flashing, "we

found him to be full of sauce. The rogue did not tell us who he was until today! Pretended to be a simple soldier with questionable relatives. Well, not you, sir, but the cousin, Wilfred."

"Walter," Adrian corrected.

"We may not forgive him for this deception." Letty frowned. "Unless he needs us to defeat the criminals."

Uncle laughed, his noble face merry. "I see you are well defended, Adrian."

"They are still of invaluable aid. More to the point, I wager the killer was likely hired by Walter, and then the man was dispatched to do for me."

Uncle glowered, showing an edge of his famous wrath. "Walter, that lizard. Then Dalton's death was no accident?"

"I think not and mean to find out."

Adrian glanced at Bia. How sweet her face, how beguiling her figure, how sharp her temper. He would bring her back to him, like she had been last night in the kitchen. Tenderly washing him, giving him kisses. He absolutely had to have more, so she must not escape him.

Bia, humiliated and embarrassed in seven directions, would have liked to smack Adrian. Forced to contend with this uncle, a duke, for the love of heaven. The final blow in a series of unexpected, unsettling events. The man, a distinguished, sandy-haired, lanky gentleman of great presence, glittered with importance. His eyes were blue, but a different blue from Adrian's. The man's chiseled features were refined, with a straight nose, high cheekbones, and a pleasant mouth. His garments were costly and in the best of taste.

Her clothing felt shabby, her hair unkempt. Bia

was not prepared for this. She marshalled her courage to stand up and leave, but in sauntered the butler.

He announced in ringing tones, "Your Grace, my lord, ladies, luncheon is served."

Now she was trapped. Everyone else registered glee at the prospect.

His uncle downed the brandy. "Excellent, I am famished. Miss Letty," he said, standing, "may I see you in?" He offered an elegant arm, and Letty, bless her, took it in stride.

"Indeed, Your Grace. I, too, am hungry. Our cook has had us on a regimen of ham, day in and day out."

They strolled away. Bia hung back, but Adrian came to her side.

"Bia, I apologize for all this upheaval. Will you dine at my table?"

She could not think what to say.

"I am so glad you are here; it means everything to me." Closer still, he whispered, "Do not go away. Say you will not leave me in the lurch."

"You rascal," she hissed.

"Yes, but you will forgive me. Come, they are waiting, and after, we must talk."

She took his arm. Little did he know, after she ate his blasted food, she would hurry away. They crossed the foyer and down the hallway, he led her into the dining room. Letty, mistress of any situation, was holding court like Queen Mary, the duke showing her a dented shield hanging on the white plaster wall.

Bia glanced about at the marble tiled floor, the timbered ceiling high above, and the ancient armaments hung about. An old tapestry scene, the colors still vibrant, of what looked like a medieval banquet hung in state. The space was huge, polished, ancient, and intimidating.

The duke took the chair at the head of the gleaming mahogany table. Adrian took a chair on the gentleman's right hand, maids dashing about. Letty sat on His Grace's other side. A footman held the chair next to Adrian, and Bia sat down.

A pretty maid served a clear soup. She tentatively tasted it. Delicious. They all ate.

"What do you write about, Miss Letty?" His Grace asked.

Bia cringed. *Please, not the dueling mistresses.*

"Oh, of adventure and romance. My hero is a duke, as a matter of fact. I chose that rank because princes have no freedom, hemmed in by rules and protocol. Dukes can do as they like. Is that not so?"

The duke's soft blue eyes twinkled. "Well, now and then. However, I must contend with an amount of duty and responsibility. Many depend on me." He winked at Adrian. "I might suggest you consider a dashing earl. There, a young man has a title, sufficient possessions, and boundless freedom."

Bia knew he hinted at his deceptive nephew. Of all the devilish things for Adrian to have done, not being forthright. Of course, he was not yet an earl, but he would be, however that got done. Like a schoolgirl, she had been hugely impressed by nothing but an army captain. She burned with indignation. He'd known all along he was out of her reach. She had not had a chance with him, not ever. Had built up a big, fluffy dream and been stupid. She would hate him eternally.

Plates of a chicken something arrived, with hothouse asparagus, and whipped potatoes. As well, a dish of seasoned peas and fresh bread and butter. Not yet done, a footman poured a white wine, then stepped back.

All this time, Adrian murmured greetings to the servants, who beamed cheerfully, obviously glad to see him back from the dead. And how right he looked in this room, in this house. No more the wounded soldier in borrowed clothes. Bia poked at her chicken, a rolled breast filet stuffed with mushrooms. She bit in and chewed. Amazing. And this was only lunch.

Adrian leaned over and murmured, "Like your meal?"

"Well, it is not ham."

He smiled charmingly. "I adore you, Bia. All day I have wanted to say so."

She ate the asparagus tips. "Now you have and can relax."

"Is that not right, Bia?" Letty asked.

She had no idea what had been said. "Pardon?"

"That, when unencumbered, we intend to go to Bath."

That uninviting idea. "Oh, I…perhaps we should go to Italy, after all."

"More promising, mayhap," the duke mused. "In Bath, you can hear bones creak, and you ladies are in the bloom of youth."

"Italy!" Letty exclaimed. "Think what I could learn there."

"I would put you on a leash, you adventurous girl, like Woof," Bia promised.

"Mercy, where did he go?" Her sister bent to look under her chair. "There you are. Behave, Woof. Good dog."

His tail thumped the floor.

"You do not need to go abroad," Adrian declared. "Why not try London?"

"We are likely too poor for London," Letty mused, lifting her glass, "but in Italy we could live on wine and cheese."

Bia shook her head. "Until we were too poor for that. I begin to think we should stay where we are, in Dover. There, we know what is what, and our funds are secure."

Letty smiled, undaunted. "If we must. Until I become wealthy and renowned with my book. Mmmm. This is a divine luncheon."

Everyone was having a blasted fine time. Bia's spirits sank to her boots. Back to Dover, where nothing would ever happen. Ships would come and go, but she would not be on them. And no one would sail in to find her. She had no way to make Letty's dreams come true, either. The future was murky, and it was all his fault. She had almost grown used to her life. Had made a kind of peace, and then Adrian had come along to knock it all hollow.

Trivial Bath and everything, the shabby little cottage, the old sofa he had bled on. What must he have thought of them? She had made a fool of herself, had put on his clothes, and would never get over having done it. Had seen his bare feet. His very knees were etched into her memory. Regret began to get the better of her irritation.

"Bia," Adrian whispered. Below the table, he took a fold of her gown in his fingers. "Forgive me."

Must be done with this! "I have. Do not concern yourself. All is well."

The footmen cleared the dishes and served dessert, a bowl of lemon ice, and very thin ginger crisps.

"Too delicious," Letty enthused. "What treaties were you seeing to, Your Grace?"

The duke launched into a loose description of what must have been complex dealings. Bia spooned up the ice, so unusual to have. Close beside her, Adrian was breathing and thinking and living. It was almost too much to endure.

The more Bia rebuffed him, the lustier Adrian became. He had absorbed the last few days into his being, but he was still him, the man he had been before the war. Home again, healing, he wanted this woman. He ate the ice, freezing his teeth.

They left the table and ambled back to the drawing room. Coffee arrived and Adrian asked, "Will you pour, Bia?"

She did this gracefully, and Letty handed cups around.

"You must see the library, Bia," her sister said, "if there is a moment before we go. Shelves and shelves, old and new. Novels, picture books on travel and exotic places. It would take years to absorb so much knowledge." She turned to the duke. "We have a library in Dover. It contains eighty and four books and pamphlets. I have counted them and read nearly all. Excepting the ones concerning navigation."

"What an extraordinary girl you are, Miss Letty," the man remarked. "You are a scholar."

"No, Your Grace. To be a scholar, I would have to know about a subject thoroughly, and I do not. I am an amateur at life. So far."

Bia regarded her sister, possibly amazed to hear

this erudition. Truly, Adrian reckoned, Letty should have a tutor. Maybe two.

Woof walked to the middle of the floor and almost hummed.

"Oh," Bia said, rising. "I will take Woof out."

Woof turned in circles.

"Come along, dog." She hurried away.

Adrian rose and started after her, as Letty asked, "Are mistresses common among dukes, Your Grace?"

Bia was already through the front door, Rodgers gazing after her.

Adrian hastened outside. "Wait," he called.

She kept walking. In a few steps, he caught up. Woof nosed through the flower beds and inspected bushes.

"We will leave when Woof is satisfied," Bia announced. "I thank you for the lunch, and your home is splendid, as you know. I am sure everything will work out for you with your cousin and so on. And do not forget to go on Tuesday to see Doctor Fox." She strolled on. "Here, Woof!"

He followed. "So. You are going to run away from me?"

"That is not…I have no business here."

"I am here."

"You certainly are. Come, Woof, blast it!"

Adrian was glad the dog had disappeared. How lovely Bia was in the afternoon sunshine. It brought out the red highlights in her hair. But she had only her thin gown. "You should have your coat."

"I am fine. Where has that dog gotten to? Woof?"

"You are cold," he said stepping next to her.

She narrowed her green eyes.

"I can make you warm," he said, putting his good arm around her. He slowly raised the other hand to caress her cheek.

She moved away. "Oh, marvelous. I can see it all now. You can come and visit me in my tumbledown cottage, Your Lordship. We can sit in the sun and hold hands."

"Great! Will you sleep in my bed, like Granny?"

"No, and you will not sleep in mine. It is my cottage."

He held her tighter, the little temptress.

"Do not hurt your shoulder," she warned.

He nuzzled her captivating ear. "Beautiful Bianca, my personal angel." That rosy mouth, her eyes, everything in her mind, her clothes, her thoughts, and dreams. He wanted it all and kissed her lips.

She still edged away from him. "This is only a thing of the moment to you, Adrian. Stop, now. You are home and a different man, I find."

"No, I am the same. Chastened, scarred, but the same. I want you with me."

"Best develop a cough. To fool your wife."

"What wife?"

"The one you will choose. The proper one."

"Bia, are you going to start all that rank nonsense? Put me in a slot, like everyone else? We had something different." He fixed her with a glance. "Maybe you did not mean any of it. Maybe you were just fooling with a fellow you found in the snow. Who was of no consequence, just somebody you could ogle?"

"Ogle?" she cried.

"You had my clothes off in a trice."

Bia raised her hand as if to strike him but did not.

Instead, she smoothed her gown and composed herself. "Yes, but I soon discovered there was nothing to see. Here, Woof! Here, boy!"

With that, she moved off, searching for the beast. Bia was fibbing. He had garnered praise for his outstanding equipment, damn her. He grinned to himself. She loved him; he was positive. It was only a matter of time until she was his.

"Here, Woof!" he called. "Here, dog!"

****

Bia went around the side of the house, glancing through windows at splendid rooms, furnished in grand style. In her mind, the cottage shrank to a hovel. She was wracked with shame, as though her threadbare underclothes had been exposed in public.

The insane dog had gone almost to the stable block to harry a procession of geese. This unwise decision resulted in an energetic beating of wings and a chase by a very large gander. Woof tucked tail and ran, the gander in pursuit, squawking loudly. The dog reached them and hid behind her skirt. Adrian laughed. Woof was so alarmed and surprised, she laughed, too. The insulted gander rejoined his flock.

Bia turned back toward the house and dared to look at Adrian. So tall and handsome, his golden hair, blue eyes, and soft mouth. Her anger and dismay vanished.

"Did you think me a terrible fool?" she asked.

Startled, he declared, "No! Why would I?"

She looked down at her clasped hands. "Our small lives, our humble surroundings. When you were accustomed to so much better."

"Bia, where do you think I have been?" he impatiently asked. "I went dirty and hungry for months on end. I slept in the mud and crawled over the land like an insect. At one time, I thought I might go mad, shot at or shelled constantly. Making decisions that cost men's lives, eating filth to keep going. You have no idea how fine your clean, warm room looked to me; how grateful I was to have your care. To rest in safety."

He took her hand and brought it to his lips. "You saved my life. You and Letty sheltered me. Not because of who I was or my station, but because you are fine human beings. Small wonder I do not want to lose you over some trifle like who said what when."

He embraced her, his arm pure comfort. "I am still that fellow you found. Just me and just you, now, this minute. Stay here with me, Bia. This can grow, can change us and make all our hopes come true. Kiss me."

She weakly resisted.

"No, do not think about it," he murmured. "Just let me and let yourself."

His lips met hers. Bliss overtook her, soaring emotions, deep longings, fright, desire, everything, immediately. His scent, his strength and kindness. The risk, the challenge, and oh, the potential. The wild thought that it could all fall into her hands. That she could swallow him like starlight and keep him always unto herself. That she was worthy of him, and all he embodied.

Bia, excited, confused, half accepted the new situation and went back to the house with him. Woof stayed extra close to her boots.

Letty came to the foyer as they went inside, her glance a question.

"It has been a long day, Adrian," Bia said. "We must go home."

"And take a bath at last," her sister put in.

This increased Bia's humiliation.

"We bathe in the kitchen," Letty chirped. "It is rustic, like camping out."

"Ha ha!" Adrian snorted. "Dirty women! I could not ask for more."

Letty giggled. Bia blushed hotly and made for the door. "Our coats," she croaked to the butler.

"Bia, darling," Adrian implored, following.

Her saved up words burst forth. "Stop calling me these…these endearments. This cannot last, it is a fairytale! All of it, from you in the snow, the horse sliding into the gully, men with rifles, citizens up in arms." She caught her breath. "I cannot think my way out of this."

"Why should you want to? It is all clear as day. If you must go home tonight, I will come at eight of the clock tomorrow morning to fetch you, Letty, and Woof. Bring sufficient goods for a few days."

"Outlandish! I will not come."

"Yes, you will," he ordered, "and best be ready, or I will bring you back in your nightie."

How imperious! "Of all the gall," she complained.

Adrian glared down at her. "Because here is where you are all going to be, so get used to it. Now the coats, Rodgers."

The butler held them out, his round face amused. Bia shrugged into hers, as did Letty.

"I have no suitable clothing," she said impatiently, tugging at her gloves.

Adrian grinned. "Neither do I. Unless old things will fit. Come in a sack. Just come, be with me, give me your strength."

Bia was torn between mad laughter and simply falling down.

"Say you will," he asked. The butler, his uncle, Letty, and even the dog waited with interest.

"Eight of the clock," she whispered.

"Eh?"

"At eight!"

To her dismay, he put his good arm around her, drew her near, and kissed her lips.

"Until tomorrow, my angel," he said for all to hear.

Bia hastened out the door, her cheeks burning. Woof ran to the chaise and his basket.

Letty skipped along at her side. "Now you are ruined, Bia, and will have to marry him."

"Nobody saw."

"His uncle did."

Bia walked faster. "That was not public."

"Does that count?"

She swept off the horse blanket and climbed into the chaise. "It does now."

Letty took her seat. "Mercy, Bia, you are no entertainment at all."

Bia snapped the reins to wake up the horse. The mare shook the harness, and off they went.

Damn and blast, she could believe none of it. The bullet to Adrian's head had affected his brain.

****

In the stables, Adrian located the steward, Burton, who had served the family most of his life. He shook the hand of the muscular, robust man.

"Thank God you live and have come home, Lord Adrian. The tenants and workers have near despaired, with no belief the viscount will keep them on at a fair wage. Or keep them on at all."

"He will not prevail, Burton. This land will never be his. To be frank, I think the bastard murdered Dalton."

Burton's jowls grew pink with ire, as the man clenched his fists. "We agreed, sir, to a man! A low, slimy fellow. Word has it he is to the ears in debt and may sell everything off. A deep gamer, it is said. He cares nothing about Marlowe lands." His face fell. "Then, with his lordship gone, the viscount's men began to come around, checking the stock and the cottages out there. Gave us all a turn."

"He is coming Saturday to take over, so he thinks, and I will be waiting to receive him. If you will round up any tenants you can reach, any workers, we will all face him together."

"We will be there, my lord, and glad of it."

"Until then, Burton. Noon was predicted for the arrival."

"Best be early, sir, to my mind."

"Good man."

Adrian hustled back to the house. By God, this would all work out. Fugate be damned, if he got the opportunity, he would cheerfully blow Walter's head from his shoulders. He and Dalton had little use for him growing up. Walter cheated at games, sulked when he lost anyway, and was hopeless at sport. Hunting, he could not hit anything, whether moving or standing still.

Dalton had not been shot, but brutalized. As sure as heaven, Walter had ordered it done. He would pay dearly for that, with his life.

Rodgers let him in. "Where is my uncle?" he

asked.

"Gone up to his rooms, sir, Clifford attending him."

"Old Clifford, still with him?"

"Aye, my lord."

"I will go up, too." He paused, hating to ask. "What happened to Posey?"

"A heart seizure, my lord, three years ago. Fast, it was, with no pain. His sister took him home to Surrey."

"I see."

Adrian climbed the stairs, remembering his old valet with affection. Posey had wanted to come with him as batman, but he had turned him down.

Nay, Posey, I will be back in no time at all, he had told the man. Because he did not want him hurt, and because he was along in years. Adrian cared for him, so he left him behind, though it had made both of them unhappy.

He went into his old rooms, still fragrant with sandalwood. The linens and draperies had been changed, but the rug was the same Aubusson, trod by his boots for years and years. Still the same white plaster walls, hung with his maps and prints of far-off places. His books were arranged on the shelves. The same bed, with its four posters, which he had practiced ringing with his hat. He gazed out the windows at the twilight settling into the trees, and a tap sounded at the door.

"Come."

A slender, reserved man entered with a brass ewer, his face familiar. The black eyes, the calm, intelligent face. Dalton's old valet, whose hair had gone gray. He would be about fifty now and, with Dalton gone, had lost his place. "Hot water, my lord."

"Thank you. Davis, is it not?"

"Yes, sir." He took the water to the dressing room and filled the pitcher.

"I remember you well. It is good to see you again. How has it gone for you?"

"Feelings have been low, my lord. First when word came you had succumbed, then Lord Dalton was taken from us. The household had little hope we could go on as we had. No one could imagine what would happen. When Rodgers told us you had returned safe, it made a celebration below stairs."

"Good times will return, Davis. I am going to see to it. You heard also that the beggar is coming on Saturday to make his claim?"

"We did, sir, and the staff will turn out in force to fulfill any need you require."

"Excellent."

"Yes, sir. Thank you, sir."

Davis departed. Adrian washed his face and hands. He had a thought to change his clothes, and gazed down at the borrowed coat, loose pants, and shirt. In the dressing room, he pulled away a Holland cloth covering garments hanging there. Such a lot of them. Fashionable in his old life, the fabrics were at the height of affluence.

His gaudy uniforms were gone. He would wear the things he had worn long ago. Time later for new clothing. Before he slept, he would have a fine bath. See to the bandage if he could. He flexed his arm and hurt shoulder. Doing well.

Adrian took a deep breath. He was home. Now he would have time for everything.

****

Bia drove in silence, her mind alternately blank, then swarming with remembered sensations. The first view of the magnificent house. The way he had been in his own home, taller, stronger, and kind of scary. Authority his, privilege rampant. He had been an army captain, after all, ordering men about. Now it was my lord this, and my lord that. Too much, it was all too much.

Adrian was only being kind, including them. Never mind all those kisses and crazy words; they would not resume. Lonesome after the war years, he would forget such nonsense. Bia snapped the reins. Surely he would not come tomorrow. He had too much to do. Oh, she grieved, why could he not be an ordinary fellow? Just her luck. Futile to think of it.

She took the lane to the cottage, and the chaise pulled around the house. Milton emerged from the barn. "Back, are ye?"

Did he not see them? "Yes, we are."

"Where be the gentleman?"

"At home," Letty said, "but he is coming back tomorrow to fetch us."

"Maybe not. Milton, the horse needs care, please."

"Aye, will do."

Woof ran all around sniffing the ground, then trotted to the house.

Quinn held the door, and they hurried inside to get warm. "Where is the fellow?" she asked.

"We took him home," Letty announced. "You should see it. It is as big as—"

"He will not be back!" Bia blurted.

Letty whirled on her. "He will, too. He said he

would. Adrian said to come, be with him, and help."

"Only in the heat of the moment. Forget it! What does he want with us?"

Letty instantly steamed. "Well. Maybe you think you are not worth anyone's time, but the duke and I had a fine conversation. I enjoyed myself. I want new things to think about. If you wish to sit by the fireplace, just go on and do it."

"Who is a duke?" Quinn asked.

"It will not come to anything, Letty. He has an empire to run."

"Listen to this, as if he is the King of Persia. He likes you! Why do you talk yourself down?"

"Who is a duke?" Quinn repeated.

"I am nobody from nowhere."

"The devil you are, Bia. We are as good as anyone, Daddy said so. Adrian is an excellent person. Everyone in Ashford adores him, did you not see it? This is not hoity-toity London. Who cares if we have no title and no money?" she shouted. "I have me!"

"I made a nice beef stew," Quinn grumbled. "Is himself the duke, then?"

"No," Letty yelped, "he is only a blasted earl!"

"Oh, well," Quinn said, turning back to the stove.

Bia burst into tears and left the room. Hurried upstairs and threw herself on the bed, which nearly collapsed it. Everything had gone wrong. She was too stupid to live. As though Fate would bring such a splendid man to her door, and that he would even think about…whatever he thought about.

She cuddled her pillow. Be sensible. Adrian was still injured and had endured much. She had seen his scars and the bullet wound. He was grateful to them for caring for him and, yes, for saving his life. He thought he had to do more, make promises, and include them. So kind of him. He was a very kind man. This thought brought a fresh fall of tears. And how would she ever forget putting on his clothing?

Letty was at the door. Woof jumped up on the bed and gazed into her face. So did her sister.

"Do not cry, Bia. I know this is all going to work out. We have a zillion ways to go. We are young, gorgeous, and intelligent. We will go back to Dover, attend the assemblies, and stroll on the docks. The war is over, so what will they do with all those handsome officers? They will be glad to know us."

"Madness."

"You do not dare to dream, Bia. Life is not a drudgery. I intend to have a good time."

"I worry how to pay for it."

"You worry, period. Since everyone died on us, you have not been the same. Where is the old Bia, who danced and sang?"

Bia blew her nose. "I sort of lost her."

"I do not think so. I saw how you looked at Adrian. How happy you were talking with him. I know you kissed him in the kitchen. And earlier, you somehow got his clothes back on while I was elsewhere. That must have been interesting."

She covered her eyes. "Do not remind me. I scarcely know how it all happened. Oh, Letty. Just days ago, we had never heard of him or the gully or anything."

"Now we know Adrian, and the duke, and we are all friends. He is coming, and we will go back with him, to stand off the invaders."

Bia had to laugh. Nothing discouraged Letty. "You are a force of nature, girl."

"And nature always triumphs. I believe the best thing to do next is have a bath. I am grubby, my new word, and too full for tea."

"I agree." Bia sat up and scratched behind Woof's ears. "Let us go and put on the water."

Arm in arm, the girls went down, the dog's claws clicking on the stairs.

Chapter Six

After an excellent dinner, Adrian and his uncle relaxed before the drawing room fire.

"Will the peace treaties hold, Uncle?" he asked.

"Everyone is desperate for them to do so, and signatures were readily gathered. There is good hope. Napoleon will be confined in deep exile, for as long as he lasts."

"If he lives, you mean?"

"Yes. He is bitterly hated, and some will not rest until he is dead. How much action did you see, Adrian?"

He swirled the brandy in his glass. "Portugal began the ordeal. Bitter fighting, guerillas to contend with besides the French. The difficult terrain, the weather that went from blistering heat to icy cold to heavy rain. I would never have believed men could march through mud. My brigade was the best, the very best." Adrian grieved, seeing their faces before him. "Along the way, in groups or singly, we buried many of them.

"Into France, plenty to do there, mopping up stragglers, taking towns and villages. At times, the people were glad to see us, then snipers would pick men off. No one could be trusted, not even us. We took their poultry, vegetables, bread, and anything else they had. It was brutal theft, but we were near starvation at times."

He paused as the memories washed over him like the dirty water he had been forced to drink.

"In '14, we took part in the Battle of Bayonne, another bloodbath. Many lives lost there. We marched on across France, taking whatever came at us. I was amazed to be able to go on slogging, preserve command, and keep myself from falling apart. Had to maintain a brave front for the men."

He told his uncle about Hougoumont Chateau and the fighting there, of his wounds and loss of memory, of his fear and desolation. Adrian was not ashamed; it had been horrific. He had seen other men break down under the strain. God bless them all. He had made it intact, until he fell.

"My boy, I commend you."

Adrian shook his head. "If I had not gone, in my pride, Dalton would not have been lost to us."

"He did not fault you, Adrian. He was proud of you for serving England. On to lighter matters. What of the Greenway ladies?"

This lifted his mood. "Letty, the writer, is a love. Bia has stolen my heart. Nay, I gave it away. She is so fine, Uncle, took me in as a stranger, out of sheer goodness. Both of them were tremendously helpful to me. I knew if I told them who I was, out would come the starch. So, as a simple soldier, as Bia termed it, we had a lot of good times."

"What happened when you told them?"

"They were damn well irritated to have been deceived. But I think I can get her to love me. Bia, that is."

His uncle smiled wryly. "You cannot get people to love you, Adrian."

"No? How did you win Aunt Louisa?"

"Persistence, abundant charm, and a spot of lovemaking that stretched her eyes. And of course, she did not mind being a duchess."

"I miss her."

"As do I. Now we must deal with that sniveling Walter. My brother's capital mistake. He was lost at sea, you know, coming back from the West Indies."

"I vaguely remember him. What was he doing out there?"

"Buying a sugar plantation. His widow promptly sold it again, deeming it foul luck to keep slaves. She left Charing years ago for Boston, leaving Walter on his own."

"Maybe she did not like him either."

"Quite possible."

"Jesus, Uncle Lawrence. We grow scant of relations."

The man grinned. "Marry the girl, build a family."

Adrian did not reply, but the notion of doing so expanded in his head to a delightful scene. To have her for his own, sleep with her, and take his meals with her. To examine her clothes and her flesh and her secrets. To truly know her. And Bia would love him. He knew how powerful that would be, if she did. It would strengthen and govern his life. He needed her love, wanted it intensely, and was determined to have it.

Uncle stood. "I must retire, Adrian."

He rose. "Very good. I will go up with you. I am so happy you arrived, Uncle."

"I am glad also. On Saturday," he said, as they reached the stairs and started up, "we will see what occurs. Will you be armed?"

"Definitely."

"Good, good. Because Walter and his retinue will likely be. I remember you as a crack shot."

"I have improved, I wager. Know that I do not want you placed in danger, Uncle."

The man shrugged. "Oh, I can still take care of myself."

They reached their floor and embraced, both of them careful of his shoulder.

"Good night, sir."

"Good night, my lad."

Adrian strolled along to his rooms to find Davis waiting.

"Good evening, sir. I thought to stay and perhaps aid you with your clothing. You are injured, I am told."

"True enough, Davis. What I would dearly love is a bath. Can that be done?"

"In moments, my lord."

"Well, call for it, and we will do our best. On your way, ask Rodgers for some bandaging and ointment, whatever he has."

"I will, sir. Five minutes at the most."

"I can wait. Take your time." He sat down in his familiar leather chair and thought of his darling Bianca. He longed to have her in the house. Tomorrow, she would come, if he had to abduct her.

****

The girls both had a bath, then in their nightclothes, ate the beef stew meant to nourish Adrian. They sat in front of the sitting room fire to further dry their long hair. Letty's hair tended to curl when damp, so she brushed and brushed until it obeyed. Bia just let hers dry as it would. It fell in a wave of its own accord.

They each braided the other's hair.

"The duke's wife died, he told me," Letty confided. "Seven years ago, of a stroke. Sudden and unexpected. He is one and forty years old."

Bia found this amazing. "My gracious, he told you all that?"

"I asked."

"Heavens above," Bia moaned.

"I told you we had a nice talk. He works with the Foreign Office and is very important. He sailed home on a British warship, the *Tempest*!"

"Astounding."

"I declare it is. What things have happened in such a few days. It is world-shaking. A week ago, we were obscure. Now we have powerful friends."

Bia gazed significantly at her sister. "Letty, he may not come back."

Her sister used her notebook to measure the length of her braid.

"I do not want either of us to be disappointed, dear."

"We shall not be," Letty confidently replied. "It will not matter if he does not come. At two minutes past eight of the clock, we will drive there for our visit and join him for the confrontation, whenever it comes. I would not miss it for the world. I am set to begin a whole new book. Now I have marvelous characters and a plot."

This fantasy could not go on! "No, we shall not, because I am driving us back to Dover."

Silence fell like a curtain. Letty scowled. "Then you will go alone."

"I am your guardian," Bia asserted, "and you must

do as I say until you are of age."

"When is that?"

Bia searched her memory. "Eighteen. Or one and twenty, I forget."

Gay laughter. "Really, such wonderful track of details my sister keeps. Well, I am going to my room to write, and you can stay here and gnash your teeth. But do consider. He cares for you. How would you like to be called countess and live in a castle? With charming and handsome Adrian Dewarr?" Letty stood, kissed her on the cheek, and left the room, Woof tagging along.

Bia sat there for a time but had no answer. She put the screen in front of the fire, turned out the lamps, and trudged up the stairs to her room. Took off her robe and climbed into the chilly bed. When she closed her eyes, she saw Adrian's smiling face. She sighed deeply, turned over, and willed herself to sleep. After a considerable interval, this worked.

****

In the night, Adrian suffered the nightmare and woke, his face and throat covered in sweat. He got up and paced around the room to cool off. The harsh details were still fresh in his mind.

Portugal. Spying on the enemy camp. The guerilla, out of nowhere, a hunting knife in his hand, plowed straight into Adrian, knocked him down with his weight, and stabbed him through his tunic. Deflected by his wool coat, the blade went off to the side. Adrian slugged the man full-force in the jaw and heard bone crack. The handle guard caught in the heavy fabric, and as they rolled in the rutted dirt, the cloth tore.

Adrian grabbed the man's wrist, turned the knife, and staring right into his face, stuck him in the gut.

Pulled the knife up hard to inflict the most damage, the guerilla shocked, blood spurting in a fountain. Adrian jumped free and escaped, five or six others in pursuit. Ran back to his men, balls zinging past him.

He dreamed of the man's abused face and how he had smelled, of rust and decay, but in the dream, Adrian was the victim. The knife pierced his flesh, molten hot, and his life drained away. He died in agony, useless sacrifice, and futility. The breath went out of his lungs, and suffocating, he woke up.

After bathing his face, he got back in bed wishing Bia were here. He could talk to her and she would understand. Forgive yourself and go on, she had said. Sleeping in her arms, the dream would not come. If he could ever sleep with her nearby, she would be so luscious.

He questioned himself. Was it all an illusion? He had not known the girl for a week. And yet, the moment he had opened his eyes and seen her, he was a goner. That all wounded soldiers fell for their nurses was generally thought, but not him. In the hospital, his nurse had been a hefty fellow who brooked no chit-chat.

No, he adored Bianca Greenway, certain in his heart it could grow. He would knock Walter in the head, take up the reins of the earldom, and marry her. And see to Letty's education. The girl had a brain.

Would Bia have him? She was proud and right next to haughty. She walked around majestically and had put him in his place a number of times. Yet she had pulled up his trousers without flinching.

When he kissed her, oh, when he had kissed her, she had come into his arms and been a perfect fit. Had softened and melted and satisfied him. Or almost. For that moment.

He cast his mind back to the last time he had lain with a woman. A century ago, in the London bed of a pretty viscountess who, as it turned out, collected young officers. It had mattered little to Adrian; he might die in a fortnight. He indulged himself, made the jaded hussy squeal, said thank you, and departed.

Adrian had not patronized the frequent whorehouses and louche women available along the march. All he needed to complete his various miseries was the pox. Instead, he drank any liquor available, since the water was vile. It had helped. Some days he had meandered along loaded to the gills. It also helped the fear. After a time, he became resigned. Let them come and try to kill him. He was ready to die.

It struck him she might be carrying a torch for the dead artillery officer. He could make her forget him, poor devil. What she needed, as Uncle had said, was a spot of lovemaking to stretch her eyes. He must see to that. A few minutes alone, if his left arm would function, then she would come to him.

He sighed with pleasure, thinking of what she would be like naked. Her creamy skin, all that red-brown hair. Her lovely smile, delicate youth, and innocent virginity. Adrian smiled in anticipation and, before he was aware, slept again.

****

Friday

Bia tossed and turned restlessly, surviving a host of incoherent dreams. Then woke, unable to remember them. She arranged the comforter and her pillows. Made mental lists of things she ought to be doing. Lay still and searched the corners of the dark room. Pushed away memories of Adrian, since he would never come back.

She dozed. Woke at a sound. Nothing there. Thought of Adrian, his long legs, the way he stood, so straight and tall. In his uniform, he must have been very elegant and commanding. Naked, he was splendid. Must not think of that.

Light began to filter in, brightening the ceiling. Taking away ghosts standing in the shadows. Revealing the chest and the chair, the mirror reflecting a growing shimmer of white, winter sunlight.

Almost another Christmas. The feeling of celebration was elusive, with no family left. Letty had not found her holly. Instead, they found Adrian Dewarr. Bia had been fearful he would not live, even before she knew anything about him. But he had pulled through.

What if he did come back for them? For her? What if everything he said was true? Dear, loving words that he honestly meant? Not fooling, or simply carried away? They had shared a few intimate moments, most unusual in every sense. Propriety had played little part in their interactions. No one was around to take umbrage, so Adrian might think…that he could have her for a mistress?

Bia immediately became offended. It was the damnable trousers! Since she had dared to do that, the rascal might imagine there to be no limits. Had he not kissed her in the presence of his uncle? Maybe Letty had the right of it, and titled men kept mistresses all over the place.

Well, he was not titled yet, however that came about. Perhaps one had to file papers. In any event, if he so much as suggested such a shabby liaison, she would deliver a sound blow to his patrician nose.

Surely, Adrian would not broach such folly. He was busy. She would say nothing until and unless he did.

That is, if he even came back. Which he would not.

It was all very trying. She got up and used the last of the water in the pitcher to bathe her face. Bia drifted to the window to reckon with the cold, clear morning, undid her braid, and brushed out her long hair. She changed her nightie for her underthings.

Noises at the door. "Come in, Letty."

The door opened, and Woof rushed in to sniff the bedcovers. Letty strolled in. "Good, you are up. I scarcely slept a wink, Bia. All I could do was plan."

"Plan?" she asked, sorting out a tangle.

"What I may do, what my role should be. The criminals will come, and that man with the rifle will be among them." With a knuckle, she rapped her forehead. "I have his face locked in my mind and mean to keep my eye on him."

"Do remember that he shoots people."

"He will not suspect me, a mere girl. Little does he know what I am capable of."

"Mercy," Bia murmured, "I can hardly bear to think of it myself."

Letty ambled to the armoire. "What shall you wear?"

"I have nothing suitable. I wore my best yesterday."

"That was not your best." Letty held out the rose wool. "This gown is lovely and elegantly simple."

Bia donned the rose gown and tugged at it. "It is a bit tight."

"No, it fits and shows off your figure. I will do your hair, and you can do mine. After breakfast, we can pack our things."

So depressing, so futile. "Letty, should we bother? He will not come."

"What if he does? Do you want to look a frump?"

Anything but that. Bia gave in and sat down at the dressing table. Woof sat beside her and, as usual, panted.

****

Adrian woke at first light and sat up. A tap at the door.

"Come."

Davis entered bearing a tray. "Good day, my lord. I have brought coffee. I hope not too early."

"No, it is fine." He took the cup. "Thank you."

He sipped. Perfection. Must get down to the kitchens. "Is Mrs. Jefferson still cook?"

"Yes, sir. All of the staff that were here when you went to the army remain in the house. Excepting Mr. Posey."

The valet handed Adrian his robe, provided water, and Adrian washed. Then he sat down to be shaved, and the man did an admirable job of it.

"I need clothes, Davis. I have nothing. I lost flesh, so my old things may fit."

"What would you have, sir?"

"I had a favorite tweed coat, gray and black. You have polished my boots, I see, so they are fine."

The valet located articles as Adrian stood and took off his nightshirt. The bandage they had applied had held through the night. He flexed his arm and shoulder. The pain had eased, and the stiffness was abating. The valet presented a shirt, and Adrian got it over his head. "Good work with the bandage, Davis."

"Yes, sir. It seemed to be healing well."

Helped into a pair of breeches, he thought of Bia doing the same for him. Was she not wonderful? The darling girl, he could not wait to see her again. These clothes, he observed, fit like he had never left. Davis got him into his boots, and Adrian regarded the glass.

The reflection wavered between himself at twenty and this present fellow. Then it became him, now, today. His face had changed. His eyes were tired and his mouth a little grim. How carefree he had been, how ignorant, going off to war nothing more than a schoolboy. No wonder Dalton had urged him not to.

Adrian turned away. The military had been full of naïve young men like him, many of whom had died. He would be forever grateful to have been spared and vowed to do good with his life.

"Perhaps a wool waistcoat, my lord? It is a cold day."

"Is the red one with the gold buttons there?"

"Aye, sir."

"I would have that." Again, Davis helped him into it, careful of his arm and shoulder. Then the old, friendly tweed coat.

"Davis, you have done well. As you know, I have lost Posey, sad to say. Perhaps you could stay on as my valet?"

The man's expression became jubilant. "Oh, my lord. I would be honored to serve you."

"Very good." Adrian combed his hair. His life was falling into line, person by person. "I will take myself down to breakfast."

"Yes, sir, and may I say how grand it is to have you home again?"

"You may, and I will see you later."

Adrian walked out and down the hallway, eager for everything to come. It would likely be an interesting day.

****

The sisters appeared for breakfast quite turned out in their fresh gowns and groomed hair. They assumed their chairs at the table, Quinn looking on.

"Right smart today," she remarked. "Goin' somewheres?"

"Back to the castle," Letty boasted. "To stay for a visit."

Quinn grumbled, "Always funnin' me. Here be your eggs."

Letty considered her plate, which bore a pinkish mass. "What is this other?"

"A ham cake," Quinn replied defensively, one fist on her rounded hip.

"The saints help me!" Letty cried.

Bia laughed. "I trust this is the last remainder of that joint, Quinn?"

"That it is. I been thrifty," she puffed. "I keep to my allowance. Just like before your grandmama passed over."

"Euphemism," Letty mumbled, pushing the ham cake aside.

Bia ate some of the eggs, but not the revolting ham. Today there were scones, and she chose one. In fact, her stomach had rapidly closed. She made do with a few bites and sipped her tea.

Letty looked very sweet in her pale lilac gown with

a pretty collar. Her sister was growing up. This gave Bia a strange mixture of joy and sorrow. Everyone moved on, it seemed, but her.

The sitting room clock sounded its feeble chime, denoting the half hour. Bia cast around for some chore she might be doing. She might go out for a walk or change her bed linens. Or the linens where Adrian slept. She had an uneasy moment and dropped her teacup in the saucer with a clatter. The room became overheated, the walls swayed. She had a strong impulse to run away from all this but had nowhere to go. She pulled her thoughts into line.

She was being perfectly silly. Everything would go right on as it had.

Letty offered a bite of ham cake to Woof. He sniffed it and sat down. She put it back on her plate and announced, "I believe we are finished here."

Bia stood. "Thank you, Quinn."

The girls fled the kitchen before the woman could berate them for wasting good food.

They returned upstairs to pack their things. Letty was full of zest.

"Do you realize, Bia, that we are going to a Christmas house party? I must write it all down!" She hurried away.

Bia had so little that was presentable, packing was no problem. She folded gowns she had already worn but could wear again. Lastly, she included the green silk gown, her best. These went into her valise with her assortment of stockings, stays, and shifts. It would have to do.

Letty appeared. "I packed all my rags. How do I look?"

"Very fine."

"Good. Let us go down."

Valises in hand, they drifted to the sitting room. The clock gathered itself, whirred, and chimed the quarter hour. Bia had never paid notice to it before today. They took their chairs by the fire. Woof lay down and groomed his paws.

"I believe my spencer will be enough today. Or should I wear my ghastly coat and be warm?"

Bia could not find an answer.

"I wish to look the part, you know," Letty affirmed.

"What part is that?" she inquired.

Letty adopted a stance, her head high. "Of a lady adventurer. Able to deal with rowdy sorts. On her feet in all situations."

"Then the spencer, Letty, by all means."

"I thought so. When I have scads of money, I will dress all in black. Or all in purple. A nice shade of purple, like lavender."

"Even your underthings?"

"No, those will be cream satin, with a delicate lace trim. What would you wear?"

"I might borrow something of yours," Bia drily answered.

"Come on, choose."

Bia considered. "A gown of yellow silk I once saw in a fashion plate. It had a cunningly smocked bodice. Then, lacy satin stays, a silk chemise, and silk stockings. I would rustle when I walked, I suppose, but they would feel deluxe. Pretty slippers to match and a sweet hat, a small one with a veil. Then I would go out driving in my phaeton."

"You have a phaeton?" Letty asked in awe.

"Do we only get clothes in this fantasy? Let us take it the whole way and make a splash."

Letty turned thoughtful. "I had not considered a vehicle."

Horses approached suddenly, making a great deal of noise. They both jumped up and went to the front door. A firm knock. Bia cautiously opened it, Letty just behind her. Adrian, looking splendid, swept off his tall hat.

"Good morning, ladies. Ready to go?" He gestured. "I brought the carriage, so you shall ride in comfort."

Bia leaned on the door jamb, worried she would sag over in a faint.

Adrian observed Bia's reaction to him. The girl had thought he would not come. But no, her hair done up in pretty waves—she had perhaps hoped. She was most becoming in her rose-colored gown and small boots.

"Greetings, Adrian," Letty said, all smiles.

"Letty. Are you set?"

"Yes, here are our valises."

"The groom will lash them aboard. Beautiful Bia. How fine you look today. Every time we part, when I come back, you are prettier than when I left."

"Oh, dear. You must go away again, so I may improve."

"Not a chance of it, my girl." He gazed into her shimmering green eyes.

"I will get the coats," Letty said, and skipped away.

He stepped closer. "I am thrilled you will come. I do not want us to be apart." He reached out and caressed her cheek. Ah, her satin skin. "Tomorrow, I will take my rightful place. If you are not with me, it will all be dross. I am back and have meant everything I have said to you."

She clasped her hands. "Adrian, about your place…"

He rolled his eyes. "No, please, not that title business again."

"But this, um, us, that is, would be unheard of. I mean, I am not even suitable to be in your company."

"Suitable to whom? Uncle Lawrence likes and highly approves of you. Here is Letty. Allow me, Bia." He helped her into her coat. She was so small. "I will cloak you in furs, sweetheart," he whispered in her ear. She remained dubious, but he would convince her.

Letty hastened past them and out the door, followed by the dog. "By golly, Bia! Come see this carriage!" Woof trotted out and sniffed the wheels.

Bia took gloves from her pocket, and they stepped into the sunny day. He would win her. All he needed was enough time alone.

"At your service, my ladies," he said. Wickers, the groom, had placed the valises securely and held the door. Adrian assisted the women in. Letty first, in hopped the dog on his own, then Bia. He called to the coachman. "Back to the castle, Shaw."

"Aye, my lord."

He forgot his injury and winced as he climbed in.

Bia noticed. "Adrian, are you in pain from your wound?"

"No, that is why I forget it. Then it bites."

"Do be careful."

Letty exclaimed over the appointments of the carriage, as they proceeded away from the house. "Such fine leather squabs and straps to hold onto. Look, Bia, a tiny vase for a flower. How stylish. And it smells nice, like lemons." She regarded the roadway as they turned toward Ashford. "I can scarcely feel a bump."

Then she sat back, obviously delighted. Adrian had impressed one sister, but it was the other one he wanted. Bia sat on his good side, so he leaned closer.

"Comfortable, Bia?"

"On your magic carpet? Yes, quite. You shall have no more hardship in your life, Adrian. Your path is charted."

"Cannot depend on that, my dear. My brother's was, too, or so we thought. The men I served with hoped their lives were before them, but many lost out. I swore if I lived, I would be bold. We cannot afford delay, must take our chances, and reach out for what we want. Time is short. Surely you agree?"

"Yes, I do. But my path is, well, narrower than yours."

"Then join mine, and there will be room for us both."

She smiled so wonderfully, he bent closer and kissed her lips. Every single thing changed. In that moment, he knew he loved Bianca Greenway and would for always.

"My, my," Letty said. "Do remember I am only a child."

They all laughed.

Their carriage rolled along the road leading to Ashford. Then to the lane and up the hill to crest it. Adrian took a deep breath. Here lay the next and final battlefield. His enemy was coming, and he would be ready. And Bia would be there to stand with him.

The carriage swept so rapidly down the hill toward

the castle, Bia's stomach wobbled. It was like flying, set free to glide like a hawk. The dog jumped into Letty's lap, which he had not done for ages, and hid his face.

"Poor Woof," Letty soothed, petting him. "We are on an adventure."

Bia's throat tightened. She had the impulse to weep with happiness as they circled to the porch. Adrian squeezed her hand, whispered, "Welcome to Marlowe Castle," and her heart overflowed.

The groom held the door, and Adrian stepped out, then held up his hand for her to take. And she did, once again enthralled by him.

They alighted from the carriage, Woof hopped down, and a footman received their valises from the groom. These were carried inside. Rodgers held the massive door, which now boasted an evergreen wreath tied with a cluster of silver ribbons.

Letty clapped her hands. "Decorations! How fine!"

Bia fondly observed her sister's pleasure. The carriage pulled away, and Rodgers ushered the merry party in, Woof included. The dog looked all around, then panted cheerfully.

Adrian's uncle strolled toward them, the picture of nobility in his fine clothes and stately manner. "Ladies, what a pleasure. You have come to join our forces?"

"Yes, we have, Your Grace," Letty said. "Depend upon it. We too, saw the man with the rifle who came searching for Adrian. Bia and I told him a bouncer, and he went away. We will know him, if he comes."

"Champion, Miss Letty." He bowed, a tolerant smile on his face. "I stand in admiration."

Letty frowned. "Oh, stop. I mean it! I have Bia's

pistol." With that, she took it out of her reticule, alarming Bia. "And I can use it."

"God above, Letty," Bia cried. "That is primed and loaded!"

"Well, it would be of little use, were it not."

"You appalling girl, give it to me."

"I must be able to defend—"

Bia snatched it away as Letty seethed. Adrian and the duke laughed heartily.

"You cannot just carry it around, Letty," she scolded. "It might go off."

"It is only small. It fit right into my bag, no one would know."

"Until it blew a hole in your foot. Just forget that idea. Mercy, let us all sit down."

Rodgers took coats and hats. Bia slipped the pistol into her coat pocket, making sure the safety catch clicked.

All went to the drawing room, warm and hospitable, the fire crackling, the air fragrant with pine. Woof lay down in front of the blaze for a snooze.

Everyone took chairs. By this time, Bia had recovered her poise. This would surely be brief. The cousin would show up tomorrow, she reckoned. A confrontation would occur, and the man would be carted off in shame by Constable Fugate. She hoped it would not be an unpleasant scene.

How splendid of Letty, Bia silently acknowledged. Carrying the pistol, ready to take on that man with the rifle. There had to be another way. The uncle was obviously the head of the family, so this Walter would weaken in the face of him. His Grace would handle it with only a few words.

Uncle Lawrence spoke. "Look here, Letty. I have found in the library a novel which may hold your interest." He handed it to her.

"Blimey! Ann Radcliffe! *The Mysteries of Udolpho*. Superb, I will read it immediately. Thank you, Uncle Lawrence."

Uncle beamed. "You must explore the library, Letty. Many enlightening things are there."

"Oh, I shall, believe me."

"Do not destroy your mind with gothic horror, Letty," Bia cautioned. "And refrain from slang, surely the sign of an inferior vocabulary."

"Oh, she is severe," Adrian joked.

"Yes!" Letty added. "At first, Adrian thought Bia was my mama."

"Not really," he denied. "I just wanted to get her goat."

Bia shook her head. "Such a bad man."

Adrian now said, "Bedchambers have been prepared for you. If you like, you may view them."

"We would," Bia announced as Letty nodded.

He stepped to the doors. "Rodgers, please summon Mrs. Bivens."

"Aye, my lord."

He returned. "Mrs. Bivens is the housekeeper. She will make you ladies at home."

This gave Bia a tremble down her spine, hoping for approval. No, no, she corrected herself. It may be the other way around.

A tap at the door. A slender, gray-haired woman of indeterminate years entered. She wore a black gown, deftly cut to enhance her figure, and carried herself with pride. To Bia, the woman was formidable, likely observed every corner of the great house, and all in it.

"Your Grace, my lord," she said in a rasping voice, and curtsied low, giving Bia a view of her intricate braids, woven about the crown of her head.

Uncle nodded. Adrian spoke. "Mrs. Bivens, my guests, Miss Greenway, and her sister, Miss Violetta Greenway, wish to see their accommodations."

"My pleasure, sir. Ladies, if you would come this way?"

Chapter Seven

Bia cast a glance to Adrian, who nodded encouragingly. She and Letty, including an inquisitive Woof, followed the imposing housekeeper. The woman was all confidence as they climbed the stairs to the landing. They turned to the right and moved along a green carpeted hallway, their steps silent.

"So wonderful to have life in the house again," Mrs. Bivens remarked. "When Lord Dalton went, the whole estate fell silent. Here we are, Miss Greenway. I thought you would enjoy this chamber." She opened the door and stood aside. Bia and Letty, Woof close behind, sauntered in.

Tall windows in one wall were flanked by dark red velvet drapes. Outside, trees thin with winter marched away. In the clear light, the pretty furnishings shone. The enormous bed sported a canopy, the silk fashioned into a patterned flower. The comforter was a softly figured paisley. The Queen Anne upholstered armchair sat upon the cushioned, deeply tufted rose-beige rug. The pale colors, so subtle and clean, were hugely attractive and pleasing to the eye.

"It is beautiful, Mrs. Bivens."

The woman nodded briskly. "Through that door are your dressing and bathing rooms. May I have a maid unpack your valise?"

Her modest garments? Bia could not bear it. "No,

thank you. I can do that. I only brought a few things."

"As you say, miss." She turned to Letty. "Will you come across the hall, Miss Violetta?"

"Yes, please." The two went away, Woof right after them, and the door closed.

Bia immediately went to inspect the spacious dressing room and was then amazed to find a separate bathing room. An oval brass tub sat on the tiled floor, and a marble-topped washstand occupied the corner. The finish of the tub floor was bumped, to prevent slips and falls, she wagered, and it stood on four gilded feet. As soon as she had the chance, she would have a bath.

Her sister sprinted in, Woof keeping up. "Mercy, I thought you had left. You should see my room! It is even better than yours and has a view; I can see for miles. How about these tubs? No more bathing in the kitchen. Quinn looking on always made me feel I was being stewed. I waited for her to add salt."

Letty talked on excitedly as they returned to the bedchamber. "I just love it here and plan never to leave." She twirled around. "But I can wait for my glory, with this existence in mind. A maid will come to attend me, Mrs. Bivens said, and what about her, too? Perfectly ageless and haunting, somehow. I wonder who Mr. B. is? Or was? Do you need to wash?"

"I would like to later and change."

"Pull the bell cord, Bivens said, and someone will come when we want anything." Letty tugged it. "Why did you not want your clothes unpacked, Bia?"

"I would bet the well-dressed housekeeper has a better shift than I do."

Letty smiled. "Dear Bia. You are such a rabbit."

"Well. A proud rabbit."

A tap at the door. Bia went to open it. There stood a young maid in black, red curls under a lace cap, a copper ewer in her hands.

"Miss Greenway. I am Edith. You likely wanted water, so I took the liberty."

"Just right, Edith. Do bring it in."

She stepped in and across to the dressing room. "Miss," she greeted Letty, went through the door, and soon came back. "I have plenty for you, too, Miss Violetta."

"Wonderful."

Letty followed Edith out the door. In the bathing room, Bia found the water in a pottery pitcher. She poured some into the bowl, took up a fat cake of scented soap, and washed her hands. Dried them with a cotton towel. In a drawer, she found tooth powder and a soft brush wrapped in a twist of flowered paper.

Bia unpacked, shook out the gowns, and hung them up, patting out creases. Then her bits of underclothing went into a drawer in the mahogany chest. This raised the scent of roses. She gazed into the large glass above it. Her things were clean and well-mended; she need not hide them. She would not do so again.

What a lot there was to learn, to be a logical human being. Much less, a countess. That would never happen.

****

Adrian impatiently awaited Bia's return. She was in his house and would be here tonight, as he was in her cottage. This time, he would not be helpless and would—

"The ladies are good company, eh, Adrian? It is a pleasure to be here. I have not had such a relaxed time in years."

"I am glad." He sipped a brandy while studying his uncle's face. "Was the war difficult for you, Uncle Lawrence?"

"In the early days, operating undercover, I had some close calls. It could be dangerous work. Once, I had to run for my life, returning from Italy into France. I was traveling on false papers, and a border guard got nosy." He looked down at his hands and the heavy gold signet ring he wore. "I had to move on from such duties. I became too well-known. I made my way home, was appointed a diplomat, and remained relatively safe from interference."

"What happened with the guard?" Adrian asked, wanting to hear the story. Uncle Lawrence glanced away and did not answer. Best to let it go.

The ladies entered, full of color and light. The men stood. Adrian's heart bumped.

"Here we are," Letty cried. "We have such glorious rooms, large and airy. They are wonderful."

"They are," Bia agreed, "with many luxuries."

"Bia would not let anyone unpack, too shy of her clothing."

"Letty," Bia complained.

"You look spectacular in everything you wear, Bia," Adrian assured her. "Did I not tell you to come in a sack?"

"I rather did. Things I brought from Dover have become worn."

"Foolishness, Bia," the duke asserted. "Your youth and beauty would shame high fashion. Even in a sack."

Bia blushed to her ears. Adrian wanted to bite her. Gently.

"Real Paris gowns, you mean?" Letty guessed.

"Indeed. I have seen them. Up close."

The girl regarded Uncle with admiration and sighed deeply. "I would not like to wear a sack. I prefer a ball gown, something diaphanous. That means sheer."

"Gossamer," said Uncle.

"Translucent," Adrian put in.

Bia laughed. "Mercy, what company we keep, Letty. These gentlemen will improve our vocabulary."

"I will take it, every bit," she said, her expression saucy. "I want to learn everything and be a Renaissance woman. They knew all there was to know."

"Because at that time, there was very little to know," Uncle corrected mildly.

"But they did not know that," Bia countered.

"Right," Adrian agreed. "If you do not know, it is impossible to know you do not know."

Groans from his audience.

"One must keep an inquiring mind," Letty posited.

"One of my professors at Oxford," Uncle related, "said I should doubt everything read or told to me. I was meant to understand only doubt would lead to questioning, examination, and intellectual growth."

"Oxford," Letty repeated with awe.

"You should have a tutor, Letty," Uncle continued, "to speed you on your way to meaningful knowledge. And to structure your writing."

Letty's green eyes widened. "A tutor!"

"To suggest reading and shore up facts. To talk with and provide you other points of view. Very valuable. I had one, and so did Adrian."

Adrian shook his head. "Mr. Drummond. He knew absolutely everything. Very vexing for a boy who thought he knew all that would reasonably be required."

He grinned, remembering. "Of course, I loathed him for this exposure of my ignorance and learned my Latin. But he prepared me for Eton, and they prepared me for Oxford, and the army did the rest."

Bia gazed at him with such affection, Adrian's muscles went weak.

Letty remarked, "I know how much I lack, so I am a blank slate. Is Mr. Drummond available?"

"Likely not, but others have taken his place, and can be found."

"To be sure," Uncle agreed.

Letty sank back in her seat, her expression thoughtful. What a fine girl, Adrian tenderly considered. He had lost his brother, but now, of all things, he might acquire a sister.

A tap at the door. Rodgers appeared. "Your Grace, my lord, ladies, luncheon is served."

Bia delighted in the day, in Adrian's nearness, and in the company. He held her hand as they strolled to the dining room. She treasured the immediacy of the moment. Every single thing in her life had altered. Her future had been shuffled like a deck of playing cards, each event changing the order.

Her chair was held by a footman, and she sat down by Adrian. Definitely, she had not expected anything like these last breathtaking days. If she bothered, she could still see that horse's rump and legs disappearing into the bottomless gully, like a judgment of the gods. If she had not been quick, she might have slid in after it. How fragile life was!

Soup, a hearty lentil, was tasty. Slices of beef were added, fresh bread, and a delicious red wine poured. Bia kept her eye on Letty, but her sister only had one glass, busy talking to Uncle Lawrence about Ann Radcliffe.

"Does she yet live?" Letty inquired.

"She does, in London, I believe. A most influential writer, much admired and praised. Her prose is vividly descriptive of her surroundings, and of course, the supernatural elements fascinate the public."

Letty's face glowed to think of this.

"Women writers are out there, Letty," Adrian added. "Critics call Radcliffe a 'mighty enchantress.' "

"Ohhhh. How wonderful," she breathed and drank her wine.

Bia felt great tenderness for her sister. "You have a gift, Letty. I know it will be realized and will do anything I can to help you on your way."

"Truly, Bia," Letty said, "you are the dearest of persons. All this last difficult year, you have done everything to keep my spirits up. I have done little but prate about my big ambitions."

"I appreciate your ambitions, Letty. And you have always been loving to me. I knew it every day." She had to wipe one eye. "I am very grateful." Bia felt the need to explain to Uncle Lawrence. "All our family, as well as a valued friend, have died in this last year. I, um, have had to learn not to be sad, to accept the loss." Then she wiped the other eye. "That had not worked so well," she admitted. "But then I met Adrian by some stroke of magic. Knowing him, I have been happy again. And today, all of us together at this holiday, is precious to me. I feel great pride that I have such splendid friends."

Helplessly, a tear rolled right down her cheek as she smiled.

At the sight of this tear, Adrian's sensibilities were

torn asunder. From a pocket, Bia took a tiny handkerchief and gracefully dabbed at her green eyes. He found her hand.

"Not to worry, Bia, darling. I am elated that our friendship and love mean so much to you. You mean the world to me."

"Hear, hear," Uncle added. "We are the fortunate ones."

Letty's face brightened. "Yes. And we have gotten by very well. Have we not?"

Bia smiled brilliantly, pleasing everyone. "True."

These were damn resilient women, Adrian believed. Nothing had kept them from going on, with little money, no family or support. He would give them security and, indeed, offer everything he owned. Sustain them in any situation. By the fond look on his uncle's face and his involved manner, he would have company there. And Bia would be his to love.

Letty, full of zest, was only sixteen. Already razor sharp, she could be brought along to achieve real distinction. Whatever she wanted, he would help her get it. And Bia was not yet twenty. It made Adrian giddy to think of her, young, untouched, virginal. He wanted to merge into her and live there. How to make this happen?

He had possibly lost his wits. Had fallen off that miserable ship in the middle of the storm-swept channel, and all this has been a dream.

Adrian gave Bia's hand a little squeeze, to prove himself wrong. No, by God, she was real, soft, giving, feminine.

He longed to possess her beyond all hope of reason, and with a great immediacy. All the struggle and deprivation of the last five years sat on him like a boulder. He yearned to break free, forget pain and death. Be soothed, comforted, and thoroughly loved. Bia was the one who can do it. Rather hasty to assume that, but he knew it with conviction. When with her, when they talked, he was enriched. To make love with her, to know her sweetness, to have her beside him, would gladden him immensely.

An apple tart comprised dessert. Adrian enjoyed a great contentment, overlaid here and there with impatience to have Bia totally his own, just the two of them, alone. Conversation wound around him.

Tasks loomed, after five years absence.

He was the Earl of Marlowe and all that went with it. Fifty percent farmer, fifty percent aristocrat. A living example and benefactor for the citizens of this area, as his father and brother had been. All those who had come to stand with him yesterday bore witness to Dewarr principles.

He had not died in the war but was saved by fate to carry on the traditions. If he had fallen on his way home, mayhem would have ensued. Walter as earl would have destroyed the title, the estate, the Dewarr name, and two hundred years of honor. The staff would have been turned out, and Walter's men would have run rampant in Ashford. No aid would have gone to the town to help the poor and infirm or those down on their luck. No funds given for the church or the schoolhouse.

Adrian glanced at Bia, and his mind eased. How beautiful she was, how gracious, whatever she was doing. With her beside him, he could achieve anything. The meal over, the party rose from the table.

They returned to the drawing room. Distant noise

was heard as carriages and wagons came swooping down the drive. Adrian stepped to the window and observed their progress.

"Who is it?" Bia asked.

"Townspeople. Doctor Knowles and others. Come, we must meet them."

She stood up anxiously. This was not her place. What would the people think? "Adrian, I should leave."

"You are my boon companion, beautiful Bianca. I need you by my side, and Letty and Woof, too." He took her hand in his. "A solid front, my girl. Come, it all begins."

Rodgers opened the door, and Adrian stepped out to greet his friends, Bia, Uncle, and Letty with him. Woof came, too. The carriages and wagons halted. Men climbed out, jumped down, and surged toward them, Doctor Knowles in the lead.

"Ho, Adrian. Word spread fast, so here we are to offer our support and aid."

"Gentleman, I am grateful." He shook hands and greeted the men, one by one. "Constable Fugate, good to see you."

The portly fellow puffed out his chest. "I am well on this, my lord, to find what is amiss."

"We shall get to the heart of it, Lord Marlowe," said Lawyer Cranston. "Welcome home."

Hearty greetings from Fisk, the publican at the Saint George, merchant Briggs, and Squire Dutton, imposing and arrogant. As well, prosperous landowners Jack Starrett, a life-long friend, and cantankerous old Mr. McCrea affirmed their backing. It warmed Adrian's heart.

"Come inside, everyone, and we will talk. I believe

you all know my uncle, His Grace, the Duke of Hayworth."

Respectful nods and greetings.

"This is marvelous," His Grace asserted, ushering them inside. "We must deal with what has gone on."

They all paraded into the house, Woof trotting to sniff everyone, and on to the drawing room. Letty highly intrigued, Bia reticent, trailed after the men and took places by the fire.

"And these two lovely ladies," Adrian announced, gesturing to them, "the Misses Greenway, found me in the snow and saved my carcass."

"What say?"

"How?"

"Sit down, everyone, please. I got out of hospital at last and crossed the channel eight days ago. Followed on my way home from Dover, I tried to evade my pursuer, but in a snowstorm, I was shot, taking down my horse. The ladies found me half frozen and saw to my wound, else I would not be here."

Exclamations of surprise, approval, and praise.

"But to more important matters." He studied the gathered men. "I believe my brother, Dalton, was murdered after word came that I had died at Waterloo. This would leave no direct heir, a distinct advantage for a greedy pretender. But the villains learned that I lived and was on my way home. Hence, the ambush."

Comments and mumbles of anger and resentment from the men.

He leaned forward in his chair. "I further believe that the shooter acted at the direction of my cousin, Viscount Walter Dewarr of Charing. For him to succeed to the title and all that goes with it, I must stay dead. But I was rescued by my friends. When Walter comes, thinking to claim the earldom for himself, I intend to confront him with his crimes."

"Oh, my lord," said the constable. "Not in violence?"

"A limited amount. I have my proof. I can identify the man who shot me and imagine him to be in my cousin's employ. I will wring the truth from Walter, who is a true fool to think he can pull this scheme off. Dr. Knowles informed me of a procession arriving tomorrow around noon. I will be here, waiting to meet it."

"The man is a bounder, my lord," said Fisk. "His crowd frequents the George. Brawlers and troublemakers, they have run up a bill that no one is responsible for."

"They throw their weight around town, six or eight of 'em," remarked Briggs, the greengrocer. "A threat to the ladies. Privileged, they are. Think they have us in their pocket."

"And him," grumbled Squire Dutton, "this tin viscount. Fancies himself. Aimed to cozy up. Gave him the cut direct."

Jack Starrett showed his vexation. "A pompous ass, he is. Lord Dalton was my friend since boyhood, and I mourned his untimely, suspicious death. He would never make such an error, eh, Adrian? When Knowles told me you lived, I was exhilarated."

"My thanks, Jack."

"With you returned, my lord," McCrea, his near neighbor echoed, "we can act."

"And we will. I am thankful to have you all with me."

"We will be here tomorrow when the wretch comes," one man stated.

"Aye, we will," others echoed.

"And not on the street. The High Street will be empty when they pass," Doctor Knowles declared.

"We shall all be here, waiting."

"That is the way."

"And rest assured, we can stand a fight," said Fisk, earning him a troubled glance from Constable Fugate.

All agreed with enthusiasm to whatever would happen.

Adrian stood. "Let us share a drop and toast our plan. Rodgers," he called. "More glasses."

Rodgers and a maid brought trays, and drinks were poured all around. Adrian raised his glass. "To my beloved brother, Dalton, whom I will avenge. I will strive always to be as good a man as he was. This I promise to him and to all here."

Everyone drank.

****

The men left in ones and twos, with polite nods and smiles to the ladies. Bia was pensive. Letty nearly floated off the carpet with excitement.

"Goodbye," she warbled. "Goodbye. See you tomorrow."

The last left, some still chatting with Adrian and his uncle in the foyer.

Bia gave Letty an elbow. "Less fervor. This may be an armed confrontation."

Her sister's eyes stretched. "Can we hope for that?"

"This is not a play, Letty. This is an actual standoff. An impasse. The cousin is ready to do murder."

"Then we must be here! To nurse the wounded, to carry water."

"You are irrational," Bia said, wanting to shake her. "This is real, not a book."

Letty became stubborn. "Books are made up of real things. I need material and experience, so do not be a stick in the dirt."

"In the mud, Miss Metaphor."

Big tears formed in Letty's eyes. Her lower lip trembled. "You mean to tear me down and say I cannot"—her voice broke—"that I will never...."

Bia hugged her sister. "Now, now. Do not cry. I hardly know what I am doing. Adrian has said, um, a number of impossible things. When he speaks, I go into a paralysis and he leads me around by the nose."

"Hmmm. You need experience, too."

Bia laughed somewhat hysterically. Carriages rattled away with more farewells and the wagons went. If she could step out, walk around, think. She moved toward the door and ran right into Adrian.

He kissed her cheek. "Bia, sweetheart, that went well, eh?"

Letty assumed a cat-like, very smug grin.

Bia gazed into his handsome face, powerless to act. "Yessss, I thought it did."

"They have a stake in what happens, and I need their loyalty. Let us sit down. Are they not good people, Uncle?"

"Indeed, they are, and fine allies. Walter is going to be stunned."

The gentlemen had another brandy and excitedly planned strategy.

"Ours is the element of surprise," Uncle Lawrence

declared.

Adrian grinned. "I allow when I step out, in the flesh, Walter is going to be shaken. I itch to kill him, actually."

"Others will take care of that, Adrian. Have no fear."

Bia listened to all this, and Letty seemed engrossed. What a time, she thought, and it is not over yet.

****

The afternoon sunlight sliced through the room. Woof was asleep upside down, paws in the air, as close to the hearth as possible. Adrian relaxed.

Bia called her sister's attention to the mantel. "Look, Letty. More decorations."

The girls got up to see and touched the evergreen boughs, holly branches wound between, the berries crimson.

Letty leaned closer to smell them. "Perfect."

"Are they not? So skillfully constructed."

"Yes. See here. The holly leaves are sharp, and very brittle. I did not know that."

"We never located the bush."

"No," Letty said, laughing, "we located Adrian instead!"

"What is this?" His Grace asked from his chair.

"We had gone out very early that morning. To see the snowfall and find decorations for the cottage," Bia began, coming back to her seat.

"He was hurt, unconscious, and in danger. We dragged him away from this horrible, deep gully," Letty continued. "After a short time, more of the snow melted and in went the entire horse! It was startling."

It gave Adrian a chill to hear it. He had cheated death once again, with the help of these two.

"We brought him home," Bia said, "and did our best until the doctor came."

"They cut off all my clothes, Uncle Lawrence," he said, looking pious. "I was scandalized."

"They were soaking wet," she explained.

"I gleaned pages of material," Letty bragged. "For instance, Adrian, I learned you were over six feet tall. Lying down, that is."

Uncle Lawrence laughed warmly.

Adrian could not resist. "Then Bia had to get me into dry trousers," he teased.

"Oh, shall you never forget that?" she scolded.

"Never in a hundred years," he said. "I was bewitched."

And the darling gave him such a heated glimpse of her affections, Adrian was enthralled.

Adrian was a rascal to twit her in company. But so amusing doing it, Bia could not be cross. He captivated her with his every word and every glance. His eyes were full of mischief and daring. When he gazed at her, she read his thoughts. They made pictures in her head of them fully together, the images hazy. She had no reality to go by, but her instincts were strong.

Uncle Lawrence was quietly smoking a sweet-smelling cheroot. It made him look dangerous, Bia thought. Indeed, he might be. Now that she had come to know him a little better, she saw he was a man of many layers. Letty was raptly listening to him speak.

"His Grace was telling me about his travels," Letty enthused. "Bia, he has seen the world and has met the King of Naples."

"Joachim I, called the Dandy King," Uncle informed them. "Groomed himself like a peacock."

"And Egypt, too," Letty went on. "The pyramids, and the Nile River." She sat back. "I am enlightened just thinking of it."

"If the peace lasts," Adrian said, "you can travel where you like. The world awaits, Letty."

The girl beamed at them all. "I would love to take passage on one of the great ships Bia and I have seen come and go in Dover Harbor. Then I would go wherever she sails, to somewhere distant and exotic. I would hear many stories and write them all down. How was Vienna?" she asked Uncle.

"Dreary and sad, I am sorry to say. Unfortunately, Letty, about everywhere I went was mired in war. The people had become drained. The great city, with all the grand monuments, had lost its fabled gaiety. But I had seen it before the fighting, when it was decked out in a thousand lights, the cafés and coffee houses merry, the people happy. It will come again, if Napoleon languishes in prison or dies. All of his devious relations, out to trade on the name, may pop up like weeds, but they will not have his power."

"Oh, yes, I will see better days if I am privileged to go abroad."

Bia sincerely hoped Letty got her chance, and that the war was truly over.

"Would you like to travel, Bia?" Adrian asked. "Farther than Bath?"

"Oh, Bath." She sniffed. "That town no longer is a goal. I would like to go to London. I am sure you know the city, Adrian."

"Let us go, ladies, at the first opportunity," he

suggested, his blue eyes sparkling. "In May or June, when the weather is fine. We will see all the sights, the Tower, the mighty Thames, St. Paul's, and whatever is at the theatre and the opera houses. You may stay at a fine hotel in a suite of rooms, and Uncle and I will escort you wherever you wish to go."

Rather an impossible idea, Bia thought, but worth a daydream. "That would be wonderful, Adrian."

Letty asked, "What else did you do, Uncle Lawrence, besides helping to negotiate peace?"

The man paused and laid his cheroot in a porcelain dish. "Well, to be accurate, I used my knowledge of languages and, in some cases, my position to achieve my ends. Which were to acquire any information I could and relay that to the Foreign Office."

"Mercy," the girl cried. "You were a spy?"

His soft blue eyes twinkled as he ran his hand through his fair hair. "Exactly."

Letty's eyes came out on stems. She held her head. "It is too much, too much."

Bia hastened to smooth the waters. "Uncle Lawrence worked to help England win the war. It was an honorable effort to listen and learn anything he might. Spying was necessary; we were in great danger."

"I do not think it a bad thing, Bia," Letty said in some exasperation. "It is just, it is so complex. I mean, how can I ever write it all down?"

Everyone laughed at this dilemma, even Uncle.

Bia enjoyed sitting in the castle drawing room with the Duke of Hayworth and his nephew, the Earl of Marlowe, now their friends. It was beyond imagination. Even Letty could not have conceived of a more fantastic setting. And the man had become Uncle

Lawrence to them all. He seemed to like the familiarity.

Added to that, Adrian vibrated with energy. Sitting beside him, Bia felt the need to hold onto the arm of the settee or be elevated bodily. All the while, he was relaxed, stretching out his long legs. She began to wonder if she could handle such a dynamic man. If he were hers to handle, that is.

Bia then thought such steamy things about what Adrian might do and what she might say, she had to take care, or burst into giggles. But abruptly, she was tired. "I think I would like to go to my lovely room and rest for a time before dinner."

"I will go, too," Letty agreed. "It has been such a fine day, gentlemen. Thank you."

Uncle Lawrence grinned. Adrian held onto her hand.

"I will miss you," he whispered.

"I will return," she answered back, and she and Letty left the room.

On the stairs, Letty murmured, "Has it not gone well, Bia? I confess I was a bit worried, would we fit in, or would they tire of us. But Uncle Lawrence is such a lovely man. So wise and friendly."

"We are fortunate to know him."

They reached their rooms, and the girls hugged. "I will see you soon, Bia."

"Yes. Come find me if you get ready first."

She went in, glad to be alone for a few minutes. To think everything over. To relish it all and take her time. Bia sat in the comfy armchair and glanced once more at the fine furnishings. In the pretty chamber, she felt secure and dozed. The light in the room gradually shifted. Rested, she strolled to the dressing room, then the bathing room. Tomorrow morning, she would request a bath in the bumpy tub.

Bia removed her gown and stays. Fresh water was in the pitcher, still warm. She took up the cake of perfumed soap, a blend of aromas, and washed. Then she cleaned her teeth, thinking of Adrian, so tall and virile, as handsome a hero as any maiden in a story would want.

A tap at the door. She hastily reached for her robe, pulled it on, returned to the bedchamber, and said, "Come."

In stepped a smiling Edith. "I came to aid you this evening, Miss Bianca. I am good with long hair. Do you need anything pressed?"

Must be upfront. "Edith, my clothes are nothing much. We are from Dover and have spent some months near here at our late grandmother's house. But we have worn out our garments in the process."

"Ever the way, miss. I think I am all right, then I find holes."

Bia had to laugh. "Well, if you can arrange my hair, I will be grateful."

Shown to the dressing table, another glass above it, Bia sat on a tapestry-covered bench. A silver-backed hairbrush lay there with a matching comb. Edith pulled out pins and brushed Bia's hair in long, smooth strokes.

The maid murmured, "Your hair has red highlights, miss. Most becoming." She inserted the last of the pins, and Edith stood back. "My, you are a lovely lady, Miss Bianca."

Bia admired her skill. "This is a treat, Edith. I look very well."

"Which gown, miss?"

"The green one, please."

She removed her robe. The silk gown went on, and the maid fastened the two small, covered buttons. The close fit allowed no room for stays. Her breasts were firm; it would be all right. The silk felt strange over her knitted stockings, half boots, and cotton shift. Bia fought off feelings of inadequacy. Adrian cared for her, so it would not matter what she wore.

"Thank you, Edith. It is lovely to have your assistance."

"My pleasure, to be sure. Enjoy your evening, miss."

As Edith left, Letty appeared. "I say, I have had my hair done, too, see?"

"Very nice."

"A maid came, Lil, and saw to everything while I lounged about. What indulgences, eh, Bia? I knew good things would come to us. I intend to get by on my brains, since I will never be as pretty as you."

"Nonsense. Do you never look at yourself? Pay attention. You have perfect skin, and your thick hair is extra lustrous, and your smile is charming. You are hugely attractive and have very nice bosoms."

Letty laughed gaily as Bia pinched her cheek.

"And you are witty and wise for the baby child you are, and Woof loves you much more than me. I predict a glamorous future for you, with handsome, titled suitors falling at your feet."

The girl clasped her hands and gazed heavenward. "Please, please," she murmured, "do not let me fail."

Chapter Eight

Adrian, attended by Davis, washed and changed, busily plotting how to seduce the delicious Bia. Perhaps seduce was too harsh a term. Tempt? Entice? Cajole? The days had become a jumble of events. The entire episode had been unique from the first. No chaperones, no formal poppycock, and he had loved the freedom of his anonymity. Intimacies had abounded so easily, he had been enchanted.

Had she not seen him in the altogether, or nearly? Held him up so he could walk, bathed him? He tingled all over, remembering the kitchen kisses. Her slim body against him, the lush feel of her breasts. He must have more.

The valet brushed off his coat.

"Thank you, Davis."

"Yes, my lord."

Adrian left the room and rambled down the hall to the stairs. If he could lure the little darling to his chamber, then, who knew? He sauntered into the drawing room, and there she was. His heart trembled.

Uncle Lawrence was regaling the women.

"There was this terrible sort of creak, and we all looked up. The chandelier pulley began to slip. We all flowed away like frightened water as the thing descended, and descended, very slowly, then suddenly crashed to the floor, hundreds of candles spinning away like fireworks. 'Bloody hell!' the prince shouted, as he was borne away by a dozen attendants. No one was hurt, but I was told Prinny made dire threats to have everyone beheaded."

The ladies laughed merrily. Uncle laughed with them.

Bia smiled up at him, and he was enthralled by her being in the house.

"Ho, Adrian," Letty greeted him. "Uncle was telling about a famous reception, at court."

"My younger days, Adrian."

He poured himself a brandy and gave a glass to Uncle. "Do not turn the heads of these innocents with your revelries, Uncle. I have been told, ladies, that this gentleman cut quite a swath through the ton, before he went off to save the world."

"I cannot endure your taking the shine off my past, Adrian. Never mind the facts. I loved the women and a party. And the prince loved me. He even offered me one of his numerous mistresses."

"What!" Adrian exclaimed.

"I declined. As they say in the navy, I had no use for wet decks."

Letty looked puzzled, then gasped. Bia blushed to her ears.

What fun, he thought, taking a seat near her on the settee. *Just room for two.* She was lovely in a soft green gown of silk, with a sloping neckline. He leaned over slightly to gain a view of her cleavage. The delicate, creamy flesh of her breasts gave him the jitters. Pressed together, they formed a crease he longed to put his tongue in. The minx was not wearing stays! He downed his brandy.

Soon she would belong to him. Tonight? After dinner? After the evening, perhaps. He would say, he would tell her...When the hell was dinner? His stomach rumbled and right on cue, Rodgers appeared at the door.

"Your Grace, Lord Marlowe, and ladies, dinner is served," he chanted, and Adrian was glad to hear it.

They took their places, Bia mysteriously hungry again, and enjoyed a fine dinner. She drank the pale wine that accompanied the baked fish, the talk at the table general, Adrian's nearness a warm pleasure. She thought of the days ahead, hoping it would all work out.

As for that, Adrian was throwing off enough heat to warm the vast room. Bia felt she was teasing a lion, just by sitting here. She reveled in his forceful desire. She, too, longed for more time, more loving, more spoken words. More of everything he could show her. Things got a trifle vague in through there, but she had great confidence all of it would be lovely. She ate peas, fascinated by racy thoughts.

Christmas Eve would be celebrated with much merriment in the household, and they would all spend it together. Letty rejoiced, and Uncle was jubilant at the prospect of a Christmas with no war. Bia was delighted at the prospect.

They consumed another fine meal, with much talk about their visitors and the looming confrontation with the cousin. Adrian was keyed up, Bia could tell, and his uncle was tranquil. Letty hardly ate a bite, she was so attentive to the conversation. Bia imagined she was writing whole chapters, all in her mind.

Dinner over, they again sought the drawing room and its comforts, the fire crackling.

Adrian sat by Bia, her face merry, as she talked to Uncle. Letty suggested a game of whist. The others agreed readily enough, and Adrian retrieved the deck of cards. They sat around the low tea table. Letty fairly threw off sparks in her intensity to win. With Bia as her partner, they took three of the four games.

"I am forced to object," Adrian declared. "You ladies have practiced and wait for unsuspecting victims."

"Of which," Uncle drolly remarked, "we are two, my lad. Nonetheless, I accept defeat."

"I was not paying sufficient attention," Adrian mocked.

"Ah, but we were," Bia joked. She shuffled the cards in a flashy way, and Uncle moaned.

"Fleeced by a pair of girls. The disgrace. I must go to my books." He stood and shuffled away to the library.

Adrian waited for Letty to go someplace. Woof supplied the reason, stood in the center of the room, and hummed.

"I must take Woof out, then I will see both of you tomorrow." Adrian saw Letty nod to her sister as she went.

He sat closer to Bia, if that was possible. They kissed, her lips warm, and his spirit soared. Every time, it was more engrossing. He could feel her want and shared it.

Bia slipped her arms around his neck and pressed against him. Such pleasure, security, and yes, sex, captivating sex. Desire sprang up in tendrils, wove around his brain and down his body like vines.

"I have missed you all day, my sweet. Things

became busy."

She considered. "I suppose that will increase."

"I have such plans, Bia, such high hopes for us, for the future."

"Well, wonderful, but—"

"Come up to my room, and I will tell you all about it."

She tilted her head. "Now, Adrian. We must be discreet, every eye is on us, you know. Letty is very sharp. The servants are watching. We will raise gossip without Letty and Uncle Lawrence nearby."

"Damnation, all I get is resistance?"

Bia just laughed.

"No privacy in my own house," he grumbled.

"Well, we are alone now," she suggested.

Adrian practically fell on her. Heat rose between them. He kissed her until she was breathless, hugged and squeezed, and Bia relished it all but slipped from his arms. "I must go. My new maid will be looking out for me."

She took his hand, and they strolled to the door and up the stairs, as he muttered curses. She must speak. He must understand her position. "I have stretched the rules of propriety just being here in your house, Adrian."

He frowned. "Blasted rules."

"And you are so romantic, it is hard to keep track. So handsome and desirable I am apt to lose my head."

They reached her door too soon and paused. "Say on," he murmured.

"I so care for you it makes me reckless," she admitted, "but I must keep your uncle's respect and set Letty a good example."

"Let me come in," he whispered.

"Absolutely not, you rogue. Think of my reputation."

He sighed. "I can readily see, woman, that you intend to lead me a merry chase."

"Oh, Adrian, you have not had to chase me far. I rather imagined I had enticed you."

"So you thought. I had a plan in place." He gazed into her face. "Thank you, Bia. For being there, for saving me from the gully and from a barren lifetime. Tell me you care for me."

"I do, Adrian, for everything you are. For your honor and integrity, manly beauty, and fine mind." She caressed his cheek. "Of course, there will always be Bath gentlemen to plunder. But I think I adore you, Adrian, every inch of you."

He soundly kissed her, hoping it would last until the next time.

Bia laughed softly. "Now, go away."

Adrian pleaded, "But Bia…" She put her arms around him and gazed up with those green and gold eyes. He relented. "All right, we will be good. But watch out, girl. I am a hungry man."

She laughed in such a seductive manner, he shivered.

"And I am hungry, too. We will find a way. Good night."

He kissed her, hoping to linger, but the door opened and she disappeared behind it. He would find a way, all right. Promptly.

She was so sensitive, so youthful. So feminine, it raised his desire for her to woozy heights. Bia was a serious girl, for all that, and considered matters carefully. In his arms, when he kissed her, she became liquid. Loved his loving and was hungry for it. Then she started thinking.

The strategy might be to attack when her defenses were down, and then…God above, he still thought like a soldier. Simply put, she must not slip away from him, or he would go berserk.

Adrian sauntered back down the hall feeling Bia near him. He worshipped the woman like a deity, but what risqué thoughts he had. He was raging with sexual fantasies. Five years in the bloody army had built his appetites into a mountain range. She would satisfy, he knew.

How had he been so fortunate to find her? An impossible series of incidents had to occur. He once again massaged his arm. His shoulder had improved.

He endured a twinge of loneliness and pain for his beloved brother. How much Dalton would have liked honest, straightforward Bianca Greenway.

In the drawing room, Uncle poured brandy and handed him a glass. They took chairs.

"Many congratulations, Adrian."

"What for?"

"Everything. Surviving the war, then finding a lovely lady."

"Bia is a wonder, eh?" He sipped the brandy. "I got around a bit, before the war. Sowed my oats. But she is everything decent and good. Beautiful, smart, and ladylike in all ways. Plus, she is a simmering volcano. When I get close, I can feel the heat. I think of sex with her and go into a trance."

"Delicious creatures, women," Uncle agreed.

"Yes, but the special ones, like Bia, soar above the

rest. Every emotion swings in, I want to cherish her and eat her alive, those sorts of conflicts."

They laughed, as men will, and Adrian enjoyed it.

"Doomed to soak yourself in love, poor chap. But all joking aside, Adrian, I consider it a gift from the gods to feel so deeply about another. I had it once, but it has not come again."

"Have you looked?"

"Not with any vigor. I have been occupied since the Battle of the Nile. Joined the Foreign Office at four and twenty. That is seventeen years, Adrian. My whole youth. Louisa's sudden death occurred while I was off spying in Naples. But the war is over for me, as well as you. I will return home to London, pick up my life, and see what occurs. I am not averse to finding someone."

"You have much to offer, Uncle."

They downed the brandy.

"I would have much to ask of anyone. But who can say? Your lady Bianca is inspiring. Now," he said, standing, "I would seek my bed."

Adrian joined him. "I, as well."

They walked to the stairs and started up.

"Thank you for everything you did, Uncle Lawrence. I know you helped win the war."

"Wars are never won, Adrian," his uncle replied. "You humiliate leaders, lock them away, and the exhausted armies go home. Everyone tries to repair their patch of earth and forget how awful it was. According to history that lasts until the next time a strongman appears and creates visions of whatever folks are looking for. Peace, generally, so there is a war for it. For land, which gets destroyed. For gold, which is recklessly spent. For the people, who are either impoverished or die in the struggle. For power, which is empty."

Adrian was sobered by the enormity of what men will do to seek control over others. "We must hold on and do our best. Speak out when we can, preserve what we have. I will do my utmost to be a good steward," he vowed.

"I know you shall, Adrian."

The men embraced.

"Good night, son."

"Good night, sir."

Adrian basked in the warmth of his uncle's affection and walked on to his room. None of his relations were left. Push Walter off the family tree, and only he and his uncle remained. Dalton should have had a wife and heirs to swell their ranks. Now, to continue the line was up to him, unless Uncle married. Uncertain, that. Paternity would not be a burden. As his wife, Bia would give him children, and he would delight in creating them. A family would grow.

How could he wait to make love to the angel? Soon, vital organs would fail. His heart would seize up. In his chamber, the valet waited.

"Davis, you have had a long day."

The man smiled, in a grave manner. "A very good day, my lord. The household cheered the outcome."

"Cousin Walter will receive his just desserts, if I must string him up myself."

"As you say, sir," Davis replied in a pleased tone.

The valet helped Adrian to undress, careful of his troublesome shoulder. The bandage was holding up. He flexed his arm. Not too bad, the discomfort was receding. He had suffered a series of cuts and random injuries in clashes and had a few scars Bia had not seen. In unclean circumstances, with little or no care, he had healed, so this pesky wound would heal as well. He had important uses for that arm.

Adrian washed and fell into a reverie of Bia's charms. Her voice, her smile, the way her green eyes could spark, then soften. He threw a nightshirt over his head, then climbed into his comfortable bed.

"It is a fine thing to have your attendance, Davis."

"My pleasure, your lordship. Rest well."

"Thank you. Good night."

The lamps extinguished, the room darkened, and the valet left.

Adrian drew the comforter around him, wondered how soon he could have Bia with him always, dozed, then slept deeply, with no bad dream.

****

Saturday

After the morning rituals, the girls descended the stairs, hand in hand.

"You are not to worry, Bia," Letty lectured. "I have every confidence. With all his friends about him, Adrian will dismiss this pretender, and the constable will put him in durance vile. Until he is publicly hanged. I must certainly include such an event in my book."

"I do not want anyone to be hurt," Bia answered. "This cousin will be taken away in shame."

"Then he will be hanged." Letty gestured wide. "Before a huge crowd of onlookers screaming for justice. I can see it all."

"Oh, give me strength," Bia muttered. "Good morning, Rodgers," she said brightly. "Are the gentlemen down?"

"They are, Miss Greenway. In the breakfast room."

The entered the sunny room, and the men stood.

"Good morning, all," Letty cheerfully greeted them.

"Lovely ladies," Uncle said with a bow. "Good day."

Adrian just smiled, and her heart twitched.

"Good morning, sir, Adrian."

He came right to her and kissed her cheek. "Good morning, sweetheart."

This flustered her, but she was charmed.

The sisters moved to the sideboard to select their meal. Letty piled her plate with kippers, eggs, and sautéed potatoes, and Bia did about the same. They took seats, she next to Adrian and Letty across from him, Uncle at the head. It gave her a grand sense of family. She had suffered losses in the past, but the gods had blessed her with new friends.

As for Adrian, he appeared vigilant. Wound up, although he chatted effortlessly with his Uncle and joked with Letty. Then he glanced at her, his gaze intense. Bia could swear he began to mentally remove her clothing and raised her cup in defense. But she could not help but smile.

He was so vibrantly male. Giving her his intriguing attention, suggesting things with his blue eyes and his grin. Things she was ready to agree to, or almost. One or two more kisses might tip her over the edge into flagrant intimacy. Just the words gave her a tremor.

She had doubts. The table where she sat was probably a rare antique. This whole house was filled with such. A whimsy, all of it! The uncle was a duke,

Adrian born to the blood, an aristocrat. Unforgettable divisions lay between them. She had completely lost her bearings, would wake up and be just her, a nobody in old clothes.

But when she regarded Adrian or heard his deep voice, she became entirely his to direct. To do with as he wished. Never mind what she thought in his absence, she was mesmerized when he appeared. Then it all made cockeyed sense. His plans, his far-reaching hopes, his passionate kisses, all seemed highly reasonable. No titles or ranks, just him and her, two people. I would be bold, he had said. How could she do less?

Uncle recounted a story for Letty's benefit. Bia scarcely heard what was said, something about two ladies falling out of a cherry tree. Letty was involved in the tale, Uncle enjoying the moment. How kind and good they were. How fortunate she was, and despite her fears, Bia was quite content.

All the while he chatted, Adrian readied himself. When a boy, Walter had been given to sudden bouts of anger and become erratic. Dalton had been impatient with such outbursts, which Adrian ignored. Walter might erupt in some way. With his shoulder lame, he would avoid blows, but be watchful for tricks.

The clock moved as they lounged in the drawing room. The hour came around at last, heralded by arrivals. Once again, wagons and carriages began to descend the hill.

Adrian rose, went to the library, and retrieved the pocket pistol stored there. He checked it, tested the trigger, and loaded two bullets into the chamber. Dropped it into his pocket and went to the foyer cupboard. There he took a plaid scarf, wound it around his neck, and put on his tall hat to partially hide his hair. Rodgers became extra vigilant, as Uncle Lawrence donned his coat and hat. Bia and Letty stood back.

"Ladies, please join us," Uncle urged.

They also shrugged into their coats, their expressions alert. Rodgers opened the massive door, and they all stepped out on the wide porch to greet the arrivals, Adrian in the lead. Clouds had blown away, and sunshine illuminated the day.

The ground about the drive began to fill with vehicles of all sorts and every kind of person. Respectable folk from town, merchants Adrian remembered, farmers and their wives. Some remained in their carriages and carts, or on horseback. Others stepped down to stand on the winter lawns. Lastly came the town elders, Doctor Knowles, Doctor Fox, Constable Fugate, Vicar Gibson in severe black, and other people he did not know.

Tenants and workers now began to come around the house. Servants came from inside. The throng around the dwelling grew. Adrian was thrilled by the numbers and the friendly faces.

When it seemed the majority had arrived, he stepped forward and raised his voice. "Good people of Ashford, old friends, and valued estate folk. I welcome you here in the name of my brother, Dalton Dewarr, the rightful Earl of Marlowe. As many of you may know, when I was reported dead at Waterloo, this good man was murdered to remove any direct heir to the title."

Murmurs rippled through the crowd.

"I believe it to be so. Though wounded, I recovered, and on my way home, a man I can identify attempted to kill me. The assassin may show up today, and I will point him out to all here."

Now there came applause and cries of yea. Probably everyone had heard his story, but Adrian was gratified to tell it. The people were glad to hear it from his mouth. He glanced to Bia, who smiled at him, pride in her green eyes.

As if timed, more arrivals crested the hill and started down the long drive. He braced himself. This was it.

Adrian took his stand on the porch. Six men on horseback came first, two by two, then a fancy carriage. This was followed by a second carriage and a barouche full of what appeared to be guests and merrymakers. Then two more men on horseback and a wagon piled high with goods, boxes, wicker trunks, and cases.

The waiting crowd on the lawns and surrounding the house were acknowledged as a white hand emerged from the carriage window and waved a large lace handkerchief. Adrian had the impulse to laugh but was too annoyed. The ass Walter thought it a welcoming party.

They drew ever closer. Adrian took two steps back behind his tall uncle and lifted the scarf to cover his lower face. The six mounted men pulled aside to let the carriage roll through. It halted at the porch, and the entourage behind went silent in anticipation. The people said nothing, just stared at them. The groom leapt down, his expression uncertain, and opened the carriage door.

God above. Walter stepped out in a yellow coat, bagged, loudly checked trousers, and red shoes, the perfect London fop. Adrian could scarcely keep a straight face. The viscount lifted a limp hand.

"Thank you all, thank you so much," he cooed in a reedy voice. "Blessings, blessings."

Folks Adrian recognized now stepped from the carriage. Lady Minnie Spencer, wealthy widow of a brewer, and her homely daughter, Silvia, both likely seeking a titled husband. Old Judge Crimmins, known to be wily, and the assassin, now dressed as a gentleman. For Adrian's supposed death, the bastard had been elevated in Walter's court. The rest of the blighters wore the viscount's blue and gold livery, confirming his initial judgement as to who had sent the killer.

Walter took Silvia's hand and raised it for all to see. "One and all, my future countess, the Right Honorable Silvia Spencer." Lady Spencer grinned, wrinkling her sallow face, and Silvia showed her teeth.

Walter now minced forward to the steps. "Uncle Lawrence, home at last? So good of you to be here."

"I would not miss it, Walter," Uncle declared, "seeing you receive what you so rightly deserve."

Walter preened. Silvia purred.

What a grasping, disgusting…Adrian had enough, loosed the scarf, tilted back his hat, and stepped forward. Walter, shocked, stumbled backward, his eyes wide in disbelief.

"Yes, indeed, cousin Walter, it is why we are all here," Adrian stated, his voice rising. "The townsfolk, the staff, the tenants and workers, and everyone else who considers you a low usurper and a cold murderer is here. They have not come to welcome you, but to witness you brought low."

Seeing Adrian alive, and publicly accused, Walter's devious face turned perfectly white. His jaw fell, he gawped. "Noooo…no, you are, you cannot be, cannot be implying…" The fool searched for words that would save him. He clasped his heavily ringed hands prayerfully. "Dear Adrian, you must listen to me," he begged, his thin voice becoming rapid. "I can explain, tell how it was—you know me, cousin!" He turned to the onlookers. "You know," he cried loudly, "all of you know I am innocent of, of, anything wrong! Anything!"

Adrian spoke on. "I say in front of those gathered here, Walter, that you are responsible for Dalton's murder, and I believe this man—" He pointed at the big, beefy fellow, whose coarse face reddened. "—did the filthy job, because he also tried to kill me."

A scuffle ensued as Walter tried to get away, shoving aside Silvia and her startled mother. Judge Crimmins gripped the carriage door, trying to keep his balance. Several mounted men jumped down to rush forward but were blocked by the crowd. Others of Walter's men were knocked from their feet and surrounded by townspeople and burly farmers. Punches, many hands, and a few kicks kept them down. It became a melee.

Doctor Knowles, Fugate, and his uncle joined the closest fray, even the vicar lending a hand. Pushing and shoving went on, and loud voices rose as the spectators milled about. In the chaos, a shot rang out.

The merrymakers in the barouche shrieked in alarm. Walter's men raucously sounded their objections. Everyone nearby shuffled away from the man lying on the ground, bleeding profusely from his upper left leg. The assassin, shouting in pain, still had a dagger in his hand, but he could not use it.

Adrian was astounded.

Bia had been absorbed in the rapid proceedings and Adrian's accusation. The crowd and its movements became unruly. Fighting broke out, and closely watching the encounter, she went rigid with fear. The man she recognized moved forward as Walter tripped and nearly fell, drawing attention, and the flash of a blade caught the sunlight. Without consciously deciding, she withdrew the pistol Letty had brought from her coat pocket. As he raised the knife toward Adrian, she flipped the safety with her thumb and fired to stop him.

He swayed and fell straight onto his back, as people screamed. The crowd rushed forward to see, Letty called out her name, and His Grace took her arm. The man bled copiously, a dark stain soaking his trousers as he yelled in rage and agony. Faces all around were appalled. Bia realized what she had done and sank into the dark.

Arms held her upright as the dazed feeling passed. Bia leaned on the duke, and Letty held her hand.

"Grab him," someone said, and others joined the cries of "Catch him! Stop him!"

Walter, terrified, had mindlessly tried to flee by running up the drive but was quickly caught. The constable grabbed him by the collar of his ridiculous coat. Though he struggled, Fugate brought him back to the house, other lawmen with him angry and hostile. Bia stared at Walter's feet in pink stockings. He had lost his red shoes.

Doctor Fox bent over the man who had been shot, then said, "He will survive. For now."

Adrian stood tall, waiting as they came. The crowd parted to let Fugate and his men through. They came at last to him, a weeping Walter firmly in hand. He again raised his voice.

"Walter Reginald Dewarr, before all these gathered here, I accuse you of the murder of Dalton Dewarr, Earl of Marlowe, your blood kinsman. The attempted murder of me and your scheme to unlawfully take your place as earl have failed. Your actions have led to this downfall, but it will be the only disgrace to an honorable name. Save your death, which waits for you."

"Adrian, Adrian," Walter implored, tears flowing, "dearest cousin, you cannot, you must not! I am innocent and can explain how it was. Just an accident, a horrible...I have done nothing wrong, nothing!" He slumped, his legs gave way, and the men had to hold him up. "Adrian, please, please," he wept, "you must save me."

The beggar whined on, but Adrian did not care to listen. "Just take him away, Fugate. The sight of him disgusts me. I will be available to testify or sign papers when needed."

"Aye, my lord. You there," the constable called to the various roughed-up riders and disgraced hangers-on. "Be gone. You are not wanted here."

The carriages and the barouche, including the wagon of goods, turned around the drive and moved slowly away. This time, there was no laughter, no triumph. The occupants did not speak or show their faces. All the riders hustled to their horses, their livery dirty and torn, mounted, and followed after them. The defeated procession traveled up to the crest and one by one, disappeared.

The wounded man was lifted into the constable's

wagon as he sobbed. A wet patch on the gravel of the drive was the only sign remaining of the skirmish. Fugate bundled a distraught and babbling Walter into the wagon, two men with him keeping guard. The villain and his wailing henchman were driven away.

Adrian turned to Rodgers, standing by the door. "Have the tables been prepared?"

"All is ready, my lord."

He called out to the crowd. "My friends, come into the house for refreshments. Please come, all are welcome."

Bia steadied as folks began to stream toward the house. Adrian took her arm and the pistol. They went inside and shed coats and scarves. He did not go toward the dining room where she could hear servants moving about. Rodgers and footmen directed people that way, but Adrian led her to a sitting room along the hall, quickly showed her in, and closed the door.

He lifted her hand to his lips. "Bia, what can I say? You have now saved my life twice."

She shook her head. "I did not think. I just acted."

"The mark of a good soldier, and what an expert shot!"

She had not quite aimed. "But—"

He bent over her, his strength, his power palpable. *Mercy*, she mused, *when he gets the use of both arms!* Then she did not think anything and sank into him like water into a sponge.

"No buts," he murmured. "I saw him move and lift the knife. You were faster. That is what it takes, love. Fast action, so you will live. That dagger could have done a lot of damage."

He held her in his good arm. "Bia, I want you to

never leave me. No more troubles, no more uncertainty. I am home, and my place is secure. I am now the earl, so I am free to say—"

A rap at the door. "Bia? Are you in there?"

She moved away from him. "I am, Letty. Come."

Letty hastened inside. "What a heroine!" she declared. "Everyone is talking of it."

Woof excitedly inspected the room, his tail wagging.

"It just took my breath, and the monster went down in a heap. A good thing I brought the pistol, eh? Or Adrian might have been run through. Come and have something. Mrs. Bivens organized a feast." Letty curtsied low. "Do forgive this intrusion, your lordship, your excellent worship. You should have locked the door." Then she danced away, Woof on her heels.

"Yes," Bia said, "I am coming." She hurried after her sister, before Adrian could say more.

Adrian cursed the missed opportunity to speak privately to Bia, but he would have another chance. What a smashing woman she was. None like her. He put both empty pistols on a top shelf.

He knew exactly what had happened. When he stepped out to confront Walter, Adrian already had his hand on the pistol, ready to fire right through his favorite coat, if necessary. He accused the murderer, saw the knife glint, then he froze. The guerilla had sprung from his dream and come to kill him! It only took a split second, only a slight hesitation, but one that might have cost his life. Then the shot had come, vibrating in his ears, and the enemy fell, the dagger still gripped in his hand.

Adrian overflowed with love and gratitude and

sailed out the door, ready to catch up with her and say so.

However, the dining room was mobbed. Everyone eating and drinking, chatting at one of the tables, or standing at a huge cask of ale, having a glass. Servants flitted about like fireflies, balancing trays. Adrian accepted a sandwich, suddenly hungry, and a glass of wine. He took a bite and had a swallow, then became surrounded by well-wishers and folks he had not seen in years.

He listened to their stories and anecdotes and reminisced about Dalton. Adrian took note of the names of their children, deceased parents, uncles, and aunts. Heard reports of rainfall and the lack of it. Discussed the church roof with the vicar and promised funds. Was jollied by Doctor Fox, who now knew his identity. His clever face was pleased.

"Would have charged two pound a visit, ha ha, but did not wish to burden your lady's purse. Fine place you have here. How is the shoulder?"

"A lot better, Doctor. Some stiffness, still. I have bathed and changed the dressing. No bleeding or redness."

"Start using the limb a bit more. Have to work through the pain. Get those muscles healing. See me first thing on Tuesday. Till then, your lordship."

The doctor sauntered away to the buffet table. Adrian searched the room but could not see Bia. They had come in his carriage, so would not leave. He turned to speak to more of his neighbors.

Letty, intrigued by the lavish buffet of hot and cold delicacies, filled a plate. Woof, too short to view the offerings, hopefully searched her face.

"Not to fret, Woof, dear, you will have a share. Look, Bia, baked custard tarts. Have some of these steak bites. Those are fish pasties, I hate them. Are you not going to eat?"

Bia placed a buttered roll on her plate.

Letty poked her. "I insist you do. It is a banquet. Else I will bang my spoon on this tureen and raise a calamity."

Bia feared she would and took one of the tarts. Then one of the steak pieces. And a jellied aspic cube with a green olive suspended in it. Very exotic.

People of all stations wandered about, some in farm or workmen's clothing, some dressed for town. It seemed to make no difference to anyone. His Grace was speaking energetically to a group of men, who hung on his words.

The two found a corner and ate their food. The aspic was tangy, and the olive sweet. They agreed the steak dissolved when chewed, and even the roll tasted extra good. The custard tart, fragrant with nutmeg, was best of all. Letty licked her spoon.

"Delicious. I am full to the top. Now I shall have a glass of that wine that keeps going by in someone else's hand."

"Take care," Bia warned, "or you will have to lie down."

"Only one," Letty promised, fed a thrilled Woof the last of her steak, and strolled away.

Now alone, Bia imagined everyone's eyes were on her. She had shot a man right while they watched. Shot him, how horrid! She would have to reckon with this, but he would live. Eager to leave, she went along the wall, out the first door she found, and into a hallway.

She tried to get her bearings. That way lay the front of the house, so she went the other direction.

Rooms gave way to other rooms, several hallways, sitting rooms, writing rooms, and Lord above, a ballroom. Four chandeliers shimmering with crystal drops ranged far above the polished floor. A line of double doors marched across one side. Bia could see a terrace and gardens. Now bare in winter, the rows went on beyond to fruit trees, knobby and stark.

She walked on, skirting the immaculate floor, to other doors. More rooms, then the library, and lo, she was back in the drawing room. People were there, looking at the pictures. Bia slipped past them, out to the foyer, and had nowhere left to go but the stairs. She climbed up to the landing and went up one more flight. There, she found an ornate upholstered chair and sat, thoroughly tired out.

This was not a castle, but a palace. Well, what would the difference be? This chair might have been a throne, from which unknown earls of old had directed their soldiers. Likely there had always been a thief like Walter, ready to attack. Those who had something were required to hold onto it.

That was what Adrian had been about. Now he had regained his home, and Walter would meet his fate, along with the murderer she had wounded. She felt no pressing regret over doing so, but maybe that would come later. Adrian had not been hurt. It had been a tiny war, and she had done her part.

Bia relaxed in the comfortable chair. How fine to be here, the quiet, the luxurious surroundings. Even if she and Letty stopped at the finest hotel in Bath, it could never be as magnificent as this house.

It had all been a once-in-a-lifetime experience, squeezed into a few days. Since she and Letty had ventured out to find holly in the snow, it seemed weeks had passed. She leaned her head back and went over the best moments. Adrian gloriously shirtless, his smile, his mellow voice. The texture of his skin. The way he had first kissed her, as if she were the only woman in the world. It carried an edge of sadness. The precious minutes had all gone by, the adventure was done. She closed her eyes and wearily fell asleep.

Chapter Nine

Adrian talked and listened, took advice, and gave some. When his shoulder began to ache, he sipped a tumbler of whiskey. Letty was amusing two young gentlemen with an obviously merry story. Woof collected pats on the head while being given tidbits of food. But as the gathering shifted, he still could not locate Bia.

The celebration began to thin. The cask of ale went foamy, and the food tables became sadly decimated. Many now began to move toward the front doors. The rooms cleared. Adrian and his uncle did the pretty, and folks left, satisfied and cheerful. Carriages and wagons slowly departed.

Rodgers and the various maids and footmen began to gather up the debris.

Letty came to Adrian. "Bia has disappeared, I cannot find her."

Adrian came to attention. "I wager she went upstairs to get a little peace."

"That sounds right," Letty agreed. "She became the object of much interest."

"You find her, Adrian," his uncle said. "We will rest in the drawing room."

Adrian took the stairs three at a time to the landing, guessed, then went on up to the next floor. There she sat, fast asleep, tenderly slumped in a big Louis chair.

The sight of her touched his heart. Her small hands were folded in her lap, her little boots together. His innocent angel, his dear love. He knelt at her feet and whispered, "Bia."

She stirred and opened her eyes. "Oh."

"You were tired?"

"Yessss." She smoothed her hair. "Of people looking at me. No one said anything, but you know, I am a stranger here."

"Not for long. Actually, they may have been in some awe of you."

Her expression clouded. "Because I shot that man?"

"Because they sensed how special you are to me and to this house. And you saved my hide once again. That deserved notice. The folks hereabout are good-hearted and will welcome you in." He absently flexed his arm. Bia was concerned, bless her.

"Do stand up, Adrian. Is your shoulder bothering you?"

He rose. "Yes. I need your loving care."

She quickly stood. "What may I do?"

"Let me sit down here. Come closer."

"Yes?"

He pulled her onto his lap. She breathed a laugh, making all his body hair stand up. "Now I am better."

"Someone will come," she cautioned.

"Likely not." He nuzzled her neck. "Mmmm, how good it is to hold you," he murmured. Adrian recalled his uncle's words, a spot of lovemaking. He would use his neglected skills. Holding her close, he raised his stiff arm and hand to caress her face. "You are the most desirable woman I have ever met."

She smiled in a playful way. "You have met many, I suppose?"

"Quite a few. But none can compare. Your light leaves them in the shade."

Bia bit her lip. This daydream could not go on, or it would become painful.

"Oh, Adrian, why do you say these things? Surely you know…that is, I have to say, to point out the facts, if you do not yet see. I have no place here and am sorry—well, that I cannot, for instance, um, become your mistress."

He dropped his hand. "Eh?"

She spoke rapidly. "I do not fault you for considering it, and as for that, I thought of it, too. Only briefly, because it is just impossible. It would set a terrible example for Letty and spoil her chances. So although I have regrets, thinking what a lark it might be, only for a short time, of course, but no, it cannot be done."

She nodded, agreeing with herself, and caught a breath. "Your uncle would be dismayed as well. And even if no one around these parts found out, there would be Rodgers and the servants, and meeting at the cottage would be unacceptable. Quinn would have a lot to say about that, and she talks. Remember Grandmama. Sooner or later, it would all come out. And seem so tawdry. Then I would have to go to Bath for sure, and even there! No, it cannot be."

Finally, she halted, and Adrian spoke. "I do not want you for a mistress."

She appeared skeptical, then disappointed. "Oh. Not even that? Blast, I have been terribly mistaken. So foolish, please let me up. Be careful of your—"

He held on to her. "I must be careful of my heart, woman, which you threaten to step on. Who said I wanted you for anything but my wife?"

She stared.

"I could never disgrace you, Bia. I value you immensely. Indeed, I am approaching a state of worship. I have lately had things on my mind, it is true, but every spare moment since we met"—he winked cunningly—"and you took my clothes off, I have been falling deeper and deeper in love with you."

"Adrian, be rational," she implored. "It is the pressure of events. The wounds you suffered, your fatigue. And such tremendous disruptions, getting shot and left to perish. Then Walter and that terrible man. These misfortunes have made everything seem, um, more urgent. You must take some time to organize your new life and recover from your injuries. This notion about me will surely fade when everything dies down."

He gazed into her beautiful, sensible face. "I want desperately to make love with you. Not for one night or some stolen hour, but all the time. I want to talk to you, hear what you say, and touch you everywhere. Buy you things, those gowns and hats you mentioned. Show you off, tell everyone you belong to me. That is what the people thought today. They know I have chosen you above any other, and hope that, if I am lucky, you will be mine."

Adrian brought her as near as he could. "I genuinely love you, Bianca. I want to consume your love and keep you safe and happy for all the years to come."

Her green eyes softened. Her rosy lips parted. Victory! He had her right where he wanted her. She would say all he wished to hear, then he would possess this woman and her every promise.

Adrian kissed her ear and nibbled the lobe. She trembled. He captured her sweet mouth and held the kiss as she leaned against him. Sought the seam of her lips with his tongue, and she gave way. He tasted her and wanted more. Her arm went around his neck and into his hair, rendering him hot all over.

"This is what I want with you, Bia," he murmured. "To ravish you with kisses, then take off *your* clothes for once, and study every part of you. While you watch me do it. Put my hand here"—he hauled it up to her beguiling breast and cupped it—"and know you everywhere."

"Oh, Adrian, you are demented," she said. "Tell me more."

"I would rather show you. Shall we go on with this? Would you make love with me?"

He had moved too fast. She became troubled.

"Now?" she whispered, her eyes wide.

By God, he must give her a smidgen of time. "Noooo, we must plan. There are conditions. For instance, I assume you are a virgin?"

She stiffened. "Well, thank you so much. Are you?"

He smiled. "I say without chagrin, absolutely not. For years."

"And I shall assume no encounters of late? At least not since we met?"

"Certainly. But to go on. Since you are, and I almost am," he stated, "if we initiate relations—"

She laughed out loud.

"Then," he continued very seriously, "honor

demands I must have your commitment to marry me. Punctually."

Silence. A chilly glance. "I should smack you, Adrian, you trickster," she admonished, giving him a push. "You have been fooling all along."

Damn, the army had twisted his mind! "No, I have not. Frankly, I was getting around your lines to strike when you were unwary. Here it is, straight out, frontal attack. Bianca Greenway, will you do me the extreme honor of becoming my lawful wife?"

She blushed, opened her mouth to say something, and he became impatient.

"I mean this, word for word, and whatever you say, I will hold you to it! When we go back down those stairs, I announce you as my fiancée, or out the door with you."

"Well! I am certain that is the most romantic utterance in the language to date. In the do-this-or-else category."

Christ, he might drive her away, he must be plain. "I am terrified, Bia," he confessed, "that you will turn me down. That I will lose you, because you do not care enough to put up with me. That you would rather go to Bath and live the high life on putrid waters."

"Ah, Adrian," she sighed. "How would I have a life, without you?"

"Marry me, Bia."

She smiled gloriously. "Very well, I will. If we can have a long engagement, with time for you to change your mind."

He wanted a firm commitment. "Wait. Do you love me? Really love me?"

"From the moment we pulled you from the snow. I

absolutely love and adore you, Adrian Dewarr, simple soldier. Or whoever you are, with all my heart."

Adrian took a small, stamped leather box from his pocket, opened it, and held it up for her to see. "Will you be my wife, Bianca, and wear this ring in promise?"

Bia was struck silent, quite overset.

"It was my mother's and grandmother's and so on, for a hundred years and more." He took it from the box. "The metal is rose gold. The central stone is a rose-cut diamond, and the smaller stones surrounding it are also diamonds." He lifted her hand. "Let us see if it fits."

Bia watched as Adrian slipped it on her ring finger. It fit very well! The gold a warm glow, the center diamond a faceted glitter, the others reflecting its shimmer. She looked and looked. A hundred years and more. It was stunning.

"Well, how about it?" he demanded.

Bia broke into laughter at his tone, the captain addressing sluggish troops. "It is exquisite. Beyond anything I have ever—oh, Adrian, can this be real? I am exhilarated and…thank you so much, to trust me with it. Your mother's? How wonderful, and it is beautiful, beautiful." She put her arms around his neck, as he grinned. "Yes, yes, to everything, you charming man."

And they kissed, Bia savoring the stellar moment she meant to remember forever.

Hand in hand, they descended the stairs and entered the drawing room. Bia mentally composed a speech, but there was no time.

"Bia has agreed to marry me!" Adrian announced.

Everyone admired the glorious ring. Even Woof took a look.

Jeanette Collins

His uncle beamed, seeming gratified. "I offer my utmost congratulations."

Letty made a sort of choked sound, almost laughed, then became quite uncertain. "Oh, Bia, are you sure? So soon?"

"Yes, Letty," Bia said, "I am. However, I have told Adrian we must not be in a rush, since he may soon find out my glaring faults."

"I cannot give her time to reconsider, Letty," Adrian joked. "We will make it. Sit down here by me, Bia, darling. Shall we call for tea?"

Letty got up to pull the bell cord, an elaborately knotted rope with a tassel.

Bia had become slightly numb. Events were speeding along, and she was swept up before them. But oh, how grand Adrian was, the light on his sunny blond hair, his blue eyes dazzling. Whatever else happened, she could never let him go.

In its way, it was somewhat too bad she would not be Adrian's mistress. That could happen right away and be exciting, to say the least. How long did it take to marry? She did not have the courage just yet to ask questions. All still a bit fragile, she must not cause any crisis.

Then she chastised herself. This was not the way. Must be bold. Bia rather addressed the air, and asked, "How long does it take to marry? What must be done?"

"A special license means no delay," Uncle Lawrence said. "You may marry when and where you wish."

"Or three Sundays for the banns to be read," added Adrian. "Then the church. What suits you, Bia?"

Once again, she was unprepared. "Why, I have not

186

thought."

"Of course, you have not had a moment," he amended.

"We have no clothes," practical Letty said. "Bia must have a trousseau."

"I will give you a bucket of cash," Adrian cheerfully offered.

Feeling trampled, Bia tried to rise above it. "That would not be proper," she objected.

"I shall like to see you in pretty gowns, my love. And, may I remind you, I am now the Earl of Marlowe, and therefore will decide what is proper."

"Oh, dear," she grieved, "it has all gone to his head."

"He shall become insufferable," Letty dramatically mourned. "But never care, Bia and I will manage everything with the monies we have."

"A special license might erase tiresome details," Adrian suggested, his voice hopeful.

"It is essential for ladies to be well-dressed," Uncle acknowledged. "Vital to a woman's happiness, I have found. I support the idea of new gowns and assorted fripperies."

"Cheers," Adrian remarked. "I agree."

Bia mentally writhed. What a conversation to have! Tea trays arrived, carried by a pair of maids, who gave her wide smiles. Oh, mercy, servants were the arteries of a household. By this time, they all knew everything.

Woof, content by the fire, unaware of circumstances beyond canine belief, panted.

The rest of the afternoon passed in a blur. Bia listened intently to the talk, then she drifted away like a cloud, trying to absorb all that had happened and all that would ensue as a result.

When she glanced at Adrian, he only seemed in high spirits, triumphant over his enemies, young and strong. Then he looked at her, so much promise in his blue eyes, it took her breath. So many secrets there, as well. He would be her lover. The thought tingled all along her spine. To her amazement, Rodgers announced dinner.

Uncle Lawrence offered his arm to Letty. Bia and Adrian followed to the dining room. It had been an emotional day, full of high peaks. She basked in a mixture of happiness and relief that it had gone so well and felt very much at ease.

They took their places at table as they had before, and maids served a beef broth, seasoned with sherry, an excellent, rich taste. Adrian radiated warmth beside her, distractingly male.

She sipped the wine and awaited the next course. Would Adrian hold her again and share more kisses? Every day saw his shoulder improve, and he became yet more completely, totally male. He bristled with masculine appetites. She had no experience, but as she often told herself, her instincts were good. If the moment came, she would be up to it. Just thinking about it gave her courage. And after all, everyone in the world had taken a leap at love and lovemaking, and Bia wanted her turn.

The main course arrived, the meal began, and every bite was perfection. Bia ate slowly, tasting each morsel.

For dessert, Bia enjoyed a slice of vanilla cake, the icing stiff and ornate in swirls. She took a generous bite. It all dissolved into succulent, sugary flavors, the cake dense yet light. It spoke to her of this wondrous time, with more to come.

They adjourned to the drawing room, and all enjoyed coffee. Adrian, fortified by the plentiful dinner, now felt ready to consume Bianca Greenway. He absently flexed the muscles of his arm and shoulder. Not bad.

Uncle Lawrence and Letty, heads together, were leafing through *The Mysteries of Udolpho* in close conversation.

Adrian edged nearer to Bia on the settee. She was so beautiful, so gracious. He scooted yet closer, keeping his voice low. "Bia, I hardly deserve you. You will not change your mind?"

"About what?" she murmured.

"Me."

"Never, I promise! But, Adrian, how uninformed I am. I mean, this huge house, how will I manage?"

"We are both taking on the estate, the house, and all in it. We will succeed, sweetheart. We have time, and we will have help. Servants stand ready to cater to your every need. And I have all the aid I require. Good tenants, a competent steward, and a secretary to give me papers to sign."

He caressed her cheek. "Every second I am not occupied, I will be at your side, my love. To show you how much I adore you. To hold and kiss you and make intense, never-ending love with you."

She blushed, exciting him, and moistened her rosy lips. He thought of nibbling that pink tongue. How the hell could he advance this affair without delay? He glanced up at his uncle. The book had been put aside.

"I am for my room, dear friends. I am still

recovering from my journey."

Woof had to be taken out, this duty performed by Letty. Soon she returned. "Arctic out there! My breath froze in the air and just hung there."

Woof hurried to the hearth and lay down.

"I am going upstairs to read this amazing book. Are you coming, Bia?"

"In a few minutes."

"See you then. Come along, Woof."

But Woof rested his head on his paws and would not leave the fire. Letty left alone.

"I feel chaperoned," Adrian grumbled, eyeing the dog.

"A little. We will steal some time."

He was immediately interested. "When?"

"When Uncle and Letty are elsewhere."

Adrian began to nuzzle Bia's shoulder, the low green gown alluring. "You must wear this gown again," he said in a low voice.

"Likely, I will. I have only a few clothes."

"I would like to see less of them."

She blinked. "Pardon?"

"On you, that is. Clothes are an impediment. I long to see all of you."

"Should I stand up?" she joked.

"You are a wicked woman, to taunt me. Can you not see I am all flaming desire?"

"Oh, Adrian," she breathed. "You are marvelous."

He leaned away. "Right."

"Do not be cross. I am trying to be, to…well, I do not know. How much is too much? What is expected of me?"

The dear innocent. "I have no excuse," he

admitted. "I am greedy to eat you up and am nibbling around the edges."

She smiled, all good humor. Adrian forgot what he was complaining about. Just being with her was glorious.

"It is very exciting to have you in the house, Bia."

"It is exciting to be here, but I know it rather stretches the limits of decorum."

"You can trust me," he insisted. "And Uncle can be very stern."

Bia laughed gaily. Adrian swept her into his arms for a kiss. It made his head reel.

"Mmmm, Adrian. You want lots of intimacies. I can scarcely keep my balance."

"Let me show you the way. First a few kisses, like this, and this—" He licked her bare shoulder. "And this," he added, moving his hand to her waist. More kisses, each one sweeter, and he put his hand on her alluring breast. The softness almost seemed to burn his fingers. Bia whimpered. His lungs locked up.

Adrian did not dare to do more, fearing she would swoon and then what? Blasted virgins were a trial. What a situation. He held her closer, relinquishing his fiery caress for a general hug.

"Oh," she sighed. "The things you do. I cannot think what to say."

"Say you love me. Seriously, we have to reach some kind of arrangement. To be together. I mean really together."

"I do love you madly, Adrian. Now I should go to my room."

"Blast and damn," he groused and stood up. "Very well, then. I will escort you upstairs, but believe me,

Bia, I am holding back my horses, so to speak."

"I can feel it, really I can."

"Then you think about it," he said, taking her hand and bringing her to her feet. "I am going to have to struggle to wait three weeks. Let us shorten the time, or my head will fall off."

They started up the stairs. "Then perhaps," she said with a crafty smile, "that license you mentioned might be obtained?"

His blood sang in his veins. "Yes! Yes, I will acquire it. I shall go to London."

"All that way?"

"I would go to the moon, to make you mine."

She smiled brilliantly. "How wonderful!"

"Oh, Bia, you are an astonishing woman."

They kissed and kissed some more.

"Good night, Adrian, dear."

Bia gazed soulfully at him, opened the door, went in, and closed it again. His lips tingled. Damn it, he had to have her for his own, or he was doomed. He debated knocking, heard the maid's voice, and walked away. He would get that license, chart a plan of attack, and soon, Bianca Greenway would fall to him like a fabulous city. Adrian hurried on to his room, humming a waltz.

****

Sunday, Christmas Eve

Bia awoke with the light, and everything that had happened in the last days rushed into her mind. Incidents crowded each other, all out of order. Snug in the warm comforter, she dozed, dreaming of Adrian. Surprised when the door opened, she sat up.

Edith peeped in, then entered bearing a tray. "Good morning, miss. I took the chance you would like a cup of chocolate."

"Oh." She rubbed her eyes, said, "Thank you, Edith," and took the cup.

She sipped the bittersweet brew as Edith bustled about. Bia requested a bath, and footmen arrived. She drifted through all of this fuss and bother, but it was worth it to soak in the bumpy tub until, terribly pampered, she got out.

As Bia silently mourned her lack of clothing, the maid revealed information.

"About your clothes, miss. You have met Mrs. Bivens, the housekeeper. She wears the best, you may have noticed, well fitted, fine fabrics. I was told by Cook that Bivens favors dressmakers right in Ashford, a lady and her two sisters."

"Grand, Edith," she replied, ruefully taking the rose gown. The maid helped her into it.

"Shall you ask that they be called for, miss?"

She did not know how this should be done. "I will speak to Rodgers."

Bia sat through attention to her hair, and Letty arrived, Woof hurrying to sniff the linens of the bed.

"Good morning, Bia, Edith. Let us go down to breakfast, I am famished."

In the foyer, they greeted Rodgers. "We have heard of dressmakers, Rodgers," Bia related, "and wish to call them in. How can this be done?"

"Write a note, miss, and I will have it sent."

"Oh, good." Bia did not know the house. "Um, where might we do that?"

"A writing room is down the hall, ladies, third door to your right."

They went that way and found a sunlit room with a

writing desk by the window, amply supplied.

"You are the countess. You write the note," Letty dictated.

"You are the writer," Bia responded.

But Letty just shook her head, implying Bia must begin to be the lady of the house. She sat down, selected a sheet of paper, dipped the pen, and began to write.

****

Adrian trotted down the stairs. Another whole day to be with Bia. There she was, looking extra fine.

"If you would," she said to Rodgers, handing him a note.

"Yes, miss, on the morrow."

She turned to him. "Good morning, Adrian."

"Good morning, sweetheart." He kissed her lips. Rodgers gazed at the ceiling.

"Hello, Adrian. We have written to dressmakers," Letty informed him.

"In Ashford. I hope that was all right, Adrian?" Bia asked.

"Indeed, it is. My lady must be faultlessly attired, and my sister, as well."

Letty beamed. Uncle joined them, and they all went in to breakfast. The sideboard was remarked on as to its abundance, and they all took chairs.

"Christmas feasting begins," Adrian happily declared, as he tucked into coddled eggs and bacon.

"We will pace ourselves," Uncle intoned, putting clotted cream on a scone, "and take exercise."

"Races up and down the stairs," Letty suggested. "Or we can move furniture and have dancing."

"No need to move anything. There is a ballroom,"

Adrian said.

Letty almost dropped her fork. "There is?"

"I forgot to mention that," Bia added. "I found it wandering around when the people were here."

"And a music room," Uncle put in. "Do you ladies like music?"

"Oh, yes," Bia exclaimed.

"More than anything," Letty exclaimed.

"Is there a pianoforte?" Bia asked.

"Indeed, there is. Do you play, love?"

Her face turned quite pink. "A little," she whispered.

"Bia is shy to play for others," Letty recounted, "but I can truthfully say she plays beautifully. Daddy said so, and I agree."

"I say, we have talent here," Adrian enthused. "I cannot wait to hear all this."

Woof, seated under Letty's chair, thumped the floor with his tail.

****

After a brisk walk about the property, the four lined up to toast themselves before the drawing room fire, hands outstretched, then they lounged in the chairs. Adrian sat near Bia.

"I am writing about a house party," Letty declared. "I need details."

"Oh, certainly," Uncle answered. "What would you like to know?"

She began. "All right. There the guests are, in some marvelous house big enough to hold them all without bumping into each other. There is lots of food and drink. Then, what else do people do to fill the time?"

"Flirt outrageously," Adrian put in.

"Kisses in hallways and alcoves, generally with someone else's partner," Uncle contributed.

The two men laughed energetically.

"Come now," Bia said, "that cannot be all, or respectable folk would not attend." She hesitated. "Would they?"

"Innocent as violets, these two," Uncle remarked. "Charades are popular, a ready chance for merriment watching each other make idiots of themselves."

"Cards and dancing," Adrian noted. "I attended a house party when at Oxford, and the host had installed a roulette wheel. I believe it was rigged, because I lost ten pounds."

Uncle said, "It was all boring, frankly. I went because everyone else went."

"What a cynical pair," Letty scolded, "but my house party is going to be more engaging than yours." She considered. "Perhaps someone may be found dead in the pantry."

"Ho, that will liven things up," Uncle commended. "Something of a plot twist."

"What is that?" Letty asked.

"An event occurs when least expected," Uncle explained, "changing the whole direction of the work. An example is in the Arabian Nights tale, 'The Three Apples.' A fisherman finds a locked chest he hopes is filled with treasure. First twist, when he opens it, he finds a dead body. Everyone looks high and low for a killer. Second twist, two fellows show up, both claiming to be the murderer. The third twist comes when the inspector finds the guilty man is his own servant."

"Mercy," Letty said. "I must do a lot more

reading."

In this easy manner, the afternoon flew away.

Bia was glad to talk and wait for the anticipated meal to be served somewhat early, the household custom. Christmas now meant so much, her dearest folk close by. All gathered here in this castle, which she trusted was not haunted.

Time passed in light conversation, and presently, Rodgers appeared at the door to announce dinner in ringing tones.

They took their places at table as before. Again, the fine room impressed her, branched candelabra on the grand table. It whispered ancient glory, and of the power within these walls. Footmen and maids scurried, and wine opened with a pop.

"Champagne, my friends," Adrian announced as a footman filled crystal glasses. Everyone raised their glass, toasted, and drank.

Bia felt icy stars twinkle down her throat. Letty seemed quite thunderstruck. Of course, neither of them had ever had champagne.

"Most refreshing," Letty remarked. "Extraordinary. No wonder everyone raves over it in stories."

"Your knowledge base increases, Letty," Uncle replied.

"I hope it all tastes this fine."

The soup course was cream of potato, very tasty. Bia sipped the wine, accepted another glass, and awaited the next course, a cutlet of sole in vinaigrette. Then more dishes arrived.

Under the table, Adrian put his hand on her knee. She could feel the heat right through her clothes. Bia studied the ring. She already, or at least almost, belonged to him, and what was the matter with that? She longed for him to possess her in complete surrender. Would he get that license?

The main course arrived to exclamations, a roasted tenderloin of beef, the surface of the meat glazed. A second wine arrived, a ruby red, as Bia hastened to finish her champagne.

Everyone ate heartily. Bubbles seemed to gather in her head, so she drank more of the red wine which complemented the meat. She had some of everything, watching that Letty did not consume too much wine. The girl was growing up. Bia did not need to keep being a mama of sorts and must let her find her own way.

As for that, her own head was floating, so she would keep quiet. She put her hand on Adrian's knee, and they shared a secret smile.

A sumptuous dessert came to the table, a rum cake with beaten cream. Bia thought it the most wonderful Christmas she had ever known.

****

Everyone relaxed in the drawing room, the talk casual, the day having been most enjoyable.

Adrian bided his time. He sat close to Bia inhaling her various perfumes, entertaining racy scenes of having her in various delightful positions.

At last, Uncle Lawrence and Letty went to the library to examine the old ivory chess set. Woof obligingly followed. Now was his chance to do a spot of serious lovemaking. He yearned to hold her and do whatever else he was able to get away with.

"Bia, darling," he began.

"I have had such a wonderful time, Adrian. To be

rid of Walter and his minions must be such a relief to you."

"Well…"

"And you have such grand friends. I liked everyone we met. Even though it was a strange time."

"Yes, yes," he agreed. "Come up to my room. I can get rid of my valet."

"You have a valet? I have been given a maid. It is very fine to have my hair done."

"Your hair is gorgeous," he murmured. "Oh, Bia, all I can think of is us being together."

He began to kiss her lips, her cheek, and her ear, and she relaxed.

"I do, too, you know," she whispered. "I think of you. Of how you were when we found you. When your clothing was gone, I had never seen anyone so beautiful."

His heart thumped. She caressed his face and ran a hand through his hair. Every cell of his being vibrated. She then put her hand inside his coat and slowly unbuttoned his vest. Adrian sat there like a schoolboy, amazed, as she smoothed his shirt.

"You resembled a blond god. I was hypnotized. But you were so hurt, I forgot all that. More than anything, I had to help you."

She actually rubbed his stomach. He tingled all over, right to his boots.

"But I remember, Adrian. I remember all of it, and I long to see you like that again."

She leaned over and kissed his lips, her hand almost, nearly, touching his trousers.

"So tall and so perfect, every part of you. And I never dreamed, never hoped I would be this close to you, with your entire self, and all you are, soon to belong to me."

She kissed him again, dissolving his brain. Adrian again took the lead, rolling her over in his arm until they reclined on the damn uncomfortable settee. His arm hurt. The gods were against him after all.

"Oh, Adrian." She laughed. "Stop. You will hurt your shoulder."

He just kissed her some more, her fine breasts against his chest.

"I should go upstairs," she murmured.

He would go crazy, must get some satisfaction, or die in agony. "I will see you upstairs, then go to my room and kick the walls."

They unwound themselves, rose, and strolled to the doors. On the stairs, she said, "I know you are impatient—"

"Frustrated!"

"—but we will have time together soon."

They reached her door. Several more hugs and kisses were necessary, but Adrian accepted his lot.

"Good night, Adrian, you sweet man. Until tomorrow." Then with a smile, she went inside and the door closed.

Adrian, the good soldier to the end, marched to his room, selected a book from his shelf, and sat down in the wing chair. Soon, she had said. He tried to estimate just how soon that would be, and began to read Shakespeare's sonnets, to get himself into a poetic, patient mood. Tomorrow he would try again, and her walls would fall. Yes, indeed, they would.

****

Monday, Christmas Day

The household settled down. Christmas went according to custom, and Adrian pined to move on. He toured the ladies through the house, explaining this and that, what various rooms were for, and who it was in the portraits here and there on the walls. He avoided the earl's apartments, wanting to surprise Bia later.

They sat for some time in the drawing room, discussing wedding plans. Adrian informed everyone that he would be going to London for the special license. There would be scant time for a wedding trip, but in spring, he would take Bia to London.

The day passed in a dream. In fact, to Adrian, time seemed to speed up.

Bia fitted in this house and into his life seamlessly. He still had trouble believing his luck. Meals were pure pleasure with her at his side. Every parting from her tore his heart, but he behaved. No one knew his lusty thoughts.

****

Tuesday

Pressure began to build on all sides.

Gilberts, Dalton's old secretary, showed up and began to prepare letters and documents for his review.

Adrian visited Doctor Fox, who deemed him healthy and on the mend.

Workers arrived to refurbish the earl and countess's apartment. Adrian spent time on the property with Burton, his steward, making plans for spring.

Three dressmakers arrived, bearing bolts of cloth and baskets of doodads. These women would return daily, and with workers coming and going, general chaos ensued. Letty and Uncle roamed back and forth, unperturbed, deep in conversation, or they spent time in the music room and library. Tunes echoed through the house.

Everything whirled around them.

****

Wednesday

Adrian escorted the ladies to the cottage, which was to be closed. The cook, Quinn, would at last leave to join her aunt's household permanently. To the girls' surprise, a jovial Milton was going with her. Their few belongings were sorted, packed up, and they waved a fond goodbye. Adrian snapped the reins and drove the chaise away, Woof secure in his basket and Bia beside him. Letty had precariously balanced stacks of books and papers, tied up with string, into the carriage seats, and it followed after them.

****

Thursday

His hallway crowded with ladders and the air smelling of paint, Adrian escaped to London to obtain the special license. Uncle Lawrence would hold the fort until he returned, the ladies closeted with the dressmakers.

Rapid progress was made to the city, the roads wet but clear. Adrian lodged for the night at White's, dined and greeted old friends, drank good ale, and gossiped, then slept soundly.

****

Friday

Early in the morning, Adrian was on the doorstep of the Archbishop's Office in Doctor's Commons, paid the fee, and left with the precious document in his hand. The traffic through the city was hectic, but the coach kept a top speed back to Ashford, the four horses stepping high. Finally, the carriage descended the hill, and his longing to see Bia grew.

Rodgers, ever on the lookout, had the great door open as soon as the carriage halted, the team stamping and blowing air.

Adrian jumped down and addressed the coachman. "Excellent driving, Shaw. Wickers, thank you. Fine job, men." He bounded up the steps. "Rodgers, good fellow. All is well?"

"Yes, my lord, now that you are safe home."

The very air changed and sweetened, and there Bia was, beyond lovely in a gown of deep blue. He stepped forward, enfolded her in his greatcoat, and kissed her with all the love in his heart. Whirled her around and kissed her again.

She laughed prettily. "Welcome home, Adrian."

The simple words filled him with happiness.

"Bia, love, I have it." He pulled the paper, covered in stamps, seals, and script, from his pocket. She stared wordlessly, her green eyes glistening.

Everyone had now gathered in the foyer. Rodgers, Uncle Lawrence, and Letty craned to see the document. "Ohhhh," Bia whispered, visibly thrilled. "It is unbelievable!"

Adrian could scarcely contain himself. "I hope all those blasted gowns and gewgaws are finished," he stated, "because we shall marry immediately."

Chapter Ten

To Bia's immense relief, immediately took several more days, but all came together. Arrangements now finalized at the church, decorations were completed in rooms she had not yet seen, and her dressing room overflowed with new gowns, slippers, and assorted luxuries. Letty walked around in a daze, her notebook under her arm. Uncle Lawrence remained congenial, and Bia had to hold Adrian off with both hands.

He was everywhere with kisses, stealthy caresses, flowers, and once, a pineapple. He wrote loving notes and left them everywhere for her to find. Still, Bia denied him entrance to her bedchamber, which he accepted with contained frustration, a degree of rage, or open laughter. And a good thing, because it was getting harder for her to say no. Adrian was captivating.

At last, the day arrived.

On a fine Wednesday morning, the third of January, 1816, they piled into the carriage. Poor Woof played dead, while Rodgers patiently petted the dog.

The carriage climbed the long hill, Adrian beside her, vibrantly handsome. Bia wore a wool pelisse of rich coffee brown with a plush fur collar. Underneath that, a gown of cream with an overlay of lace, the bosom tucked and pleated. Her underclothes and stockings were of the finest silk, her slippers white leather, and she carried a matching fur muff. She sat there like royalty.

The carriage swept down the lane and into Ashford, Adrian gripping her gloved hand. The vehicle halted at the church. The door opened and he hopped out, raised his hand to her, and Bia stepped down to the sidewalk, her pulse beating rapidly.

People had gathered, smiled, waved, and called out congratulations.

Letty, on the arm of the duke, gloried in the attention as His Grace nobly smiled. Adrian held Bia's arm and greeted everyone with ease.

The bell began to ring, deeply reverberating. Bia gazed up at the high steeple enclosing the bell, soaring above the small brick and fieldstone church. Not at all imposing, but welcoming. Wide Gothic doors, liberally studded, stood open at the top of the short flight of steps. Their party proceeded inside, and she and Adrian parted, with a long look. Uncle led him away.

The sisters went to an anteroom, removed coats, and left their things on a table. Letty, all in pale blue, began to fuss with Bia's gown.

"Oh, stop, Letty, or I will fly apart."

"Funny Bia." She laughed. "You look beautiful. I am the nervous one."

"You look lovely, as well. How long do we have?" she asked, gazing into a small mirror.

But the organ began to play a meandering tune to signal everyone to take their places. Uncle Lawrence appeared at the door and put a bouquet of white rosebuds in her hand.

"Shall we, my dear?"

"Thank you. Yes. Yes, I am ready." The music became louder. "You first, Letty."

Letty left to take her walk down the center aisle to the altar. They let a minute pass, then Bia took His Grace's arm, clutched the flowers, and strolled into her future. A little scattered, a little tremulous, she saw how many had come to see Adrian married. They went up the carpet between the pews, and there he stood, smiling, looking over his shoulder at her, tall and elegantly handsome.

Letty had taken her place to the left. Uncle Lawrence kissed her cheek, handed her forward to Adrian, and joined Letty. Adrian's best man, amiable Jack Starrett, stood to Adrian's right. Vicar Gibson lifted his voice and began.

"Dearly beloved…"

It all passed in a dream. The old words, the gold ring, the promises, the kiss, and it was over. Those who had witnessed the event applauded. Bia could not stop smiling. They each signed the registry, retrieved coats and belongings, and hastened out the door to cheers.

The carriage waited. Adrian took a pouch from Wickers and tossed coins to the onlookers, handful after handful. Children scampered, dogs barked; it was thrilling. They climbed into the coach and rolled away. It was perfect, perfect, and she brimmed with joy.

Bia had found true Christmas when she had found Adrian and would never forget it again.

****

Adrian tucked Bia's arm in his. They had signed their names in the registry book for all to see and would do so in the family Bible, so their children and grandchildren would know them. It gave him a great feeling of joining the ranks of his forebears, one of them at last, now a man with a wife.

"My countess Bianca," he whispered.

"My husband," she said, her lovely voice full of promise.

The carriage was too crowded to say more, although Letty and Uncle Lawrence were stoically deaf and blind. Get through the wedding breakfast and the few guests, Adrian mused, and then Bia would belong to him alone.

They alighted at the house. Rodgers received them, his face wreathed in smiles. Woof turned in circles. This happiness obtained as they proceeded through the house. Guests and servants alike were quick to congratulate, tease, and as one, eat and drink the house down. At table, at a buffet, and a bar set up in the dining room, frivolity went on.

Adrian reveled in his wife entertaining the guests, her mood relaxed. She was magnificent. If only all these people would go away, he could tell her. He monitored his liquor intake and ate little. He was hideously keyed up, as if enemy troops were about to overwhelm him. However, he stood at ease, waiting, waiting.

The afternoon drew down at last, and folks began to leave. Adrian bustled them out the door unashamedly, by ones and twos, Bia by his side.

As the door shut on the last of them, she laughed. "Dear Adrian, I was afraid you would blow a whistle, so they would stampede out."

"I do not have a whistle, or I would have."

Rodgers hurried away to supervise the servants clearing up. Letty and Uncle Lawrence had faded from view; Woof was nowhere in sight. By God, he had waited for eons and would brook no further delay.

"Let us retire from all this."

"Can we just leave?" Bia answered, glancing all around.

"Yes." He took her hand and led her to the stairs, his heart skipping beats.

****

Bia climbed, her hand in Adrian's, as if scaling a ladder to a new reality. She was slightly uneasy but would jump ahead into life. No waiting any longer to have her piece of personal, physical sensation. Of realizing all the quivering, shapeless yearnings she had tamped down for years.

They reached a set of paneled doors. Adrian opened them, and they walked in. Oil lamps softly lit a large sitting area, beautifully furnished. A blue and green patterned rug cushioned her feet. Lovely landscape paintings lined the white plaster walls. Comfortable chairs and settees stood about covered in fine leather and tapestry. A fire burned in the screened fireplace.

"It is wonderful, Adrian. Did you choose all this?"

"I did. But come, see your chamber. It is just there, to the right. If you will make your preparations, I will join you in half an hour. I will knock."

He held her for a kiss, his blue eyes shining, his sunny blond hair a beacon. Then he was gone. Bia went to the other door, opened it, and stepped in.

The chamber was also a luxury of space. The white walls were graced with art, the rug a deep green. On the enormous bed lay her nightie, a confection of lace and transparent silk. Edith, her maid, waited, to help her undress.

"Oh, my lady," she breathed. "I do wish you joy."

"Thank you, Edith."

Off with all her wedding finery. Bia tried to see ahead, to visualize what would occur, but could not. Naked for a moment as Edith gathered the folds of her nightgown, she shivered. The cloth, thin as it was, proved a comfort. She refreshed herself in the massive dressing room, then sat at a lovely vanity as Edith removed pins and brushed out her long hair. The large glass above it sat in a gilt frame. All of it pleased her.

The lamps shone on the fine chamber. Heavy blue velvet drapes were closed over what must be wide windows. It was all a bit unreal, and her pulse hitched as Edith gathered garments, curtsied, and left. Bia sat in an upholstered wing chair, then stood again. Glanced at the bed, covered by a gold and blue patterned comforter, turned down to expose fine linen sheets, with fat pillows stacked up.

Bia began to detect an edge of panic in her middle. The knock at the door nearly tipped her over the edge. She clasped her hands, and said, "Come."

Adrian sauntered in, the dear, darling man. He wore a red brocade robe, a contrast to his bright hair. She labored to recall what he had looked like with no clothes, there in the cottage, but he was scarcely able to stand up then. Now, he rather loomed, and she was unable to swallow. He ambled toward her, pure strength.

"Bia, love. My angel wife."

Alarm washed over her like cold water. He put his arm around her shoulders. Adrian had never seen her unclothed!

"Do you like the rooms?" he asked.

"Y-y-yes," she stammered, her throat dry. "I do."

"Sweet child." He kissed all over her face. "Now, do not get the wind up, Bia," he said gently. "We need not rush into anything."

She flinched. After all this waiting? "I want to begin, Adrian, really, with all of it. I am not afraid," she fibbed, hiding her trembling hands. He put his arm around her waist, his embrace reassuring.

"We are finally alone, Bia, and have all the time in the world to be together."

Adrian wore no nightshirt and shrugged off his robe as Bia watched, her green eyes wide, her lips parted. His heart bumped against his ribs. He moved slowly; Bia must not be frightened. His shoulder was in decent shape, scarred but presentable.

He put his fingers into her mass of shining hair. It tumbled down her back and pretty shoulders, totally female. "Beautiful, beautiful," he murmured, kissed her lips and cheeks, and put his face into her fragrant tresses. She smelled of lemons and soap and woman.

Bia ran her hands across his chest. Kissed his skin here and there, stirring his blood. Adrian pushed the flimsy gown down her shoulders and arms, and it fell into a puddle of lace and silk at her feet. Her breasts were heavy and full, the nipples pink berries. He was stunned by her beauty. They stood there, each hypnotized by the sight of the other. More kisses as he held her body against him, to feel all of her. His cock throbbed with want.

Adrian took her hand, led her to the bed, and threw aside the comforter. He gestured smartly. "Get in."

She giggled. "Aye, my captain."

"Sorry, sorry. I forget myself. Please, dear love, lie down with me and allow me to do outrageous things."

She laughed gaily and did so. Turned and lay back on the pillows, a fabled vision of a sorceress. Gorgeous, inviting, and soon to belong to him in every way he could think of. Adrian climbed in after her. Lovemaking had never been so electric, or so easy.

Christ, she was a virgin. Must allow for that. They snuggled together, a joy in itself. Her creamy, satin skin and flowing, luxurious hair, her flowery, clean scent, all bewitched his senses. But urgent need, long delayed, was gaining on him. As his cock swelled, his brain shrank. He moved in a reverie and began to increase his lovemaking. Kissed her lips until she was breathless, then turned his attention to her beautiful body.

Kissed and licked the curve of her throat. Those breasts, the nipples furled and taut. He kissed all around them, then took one bud into his mouth. Caressing the other breast, he sucked gently, drawing her essence into himself and owning it. She trembled, and he loved it. He nipped with his teeth; she put her hands in his hair and pulled.

Adrian smoothed his hand down her small belly and into her pubic hair. She bucked like a pony. He put a portion of his weight over her and moved down to the folded petals of her sex. Bia modestly put her knees together. He pushed his knee between them and began to tease her with his fingers. She laughed softly.

Then she began to do things to him. His mind revolved. Bia pulled his hair again and bit his good shoulder. Scraped her nails down his back, just enough to make a tiger of him. He growled, found her moist entrance, and stroked in the tip of his middle finger. Bia fell quiet, watching, listening.

He moved his finger in a slow circle. She closed

her eyes and arched her back. "Feel everything, Bia, let go," he whispered. He pushed his finger in farther, moved up to find the little rounded nubbin, and stroked it with his thumb. He thought she would jump off the bed, but he held fast to her.

"Aaaa-drian," she whispered.

He kept on beckoning and tormenting her. "Feel me, feel everything. I love you so much, darling, and want to love you everywhere, in every way."

Abruptly, Bia became languid. He rubbed and played her as she grew wet and he smelled her musk. She gripped the bedsheet and shook all over, her expression, her entire body, surprised. Trembled and shivered as Adrian worried he had gone too far, too fast.

"Ohhhhh," she gulped. "You devil!"

He climbed back up to hold her close. "There is more," he murmured. "Much more."

Bia had been flailed to flinders in a windstorm. She had held onto the thread of her consciousness, fighting not to slip into a pit of spinning emotional debris. Heated undulations had raged through her flesh. He had rubbed something, ruthlessly stuck her with his long finger, and her reason had snuffed out like a candle. She was torn to bits and wrenched back together, fell down and down and lost her breath. It had been riveting, and she trembled as he promised more.

Adrian gazed into her face. "You precious creature," he murmured. "What emotion you are capable of."

"Well, uh…" She caught an extra breath.

He fondly smoothed her hair. "Do not worry about anything. This is all natural and normal."

"What, you did not invent it?"

He laughed. "Sadly not, but I am expert at the game." He gathered her to him. "With you, I will achieve excellence." He boldly sucked his middle finger, shocking her. "You taste like lemon squash."

Astounded, she laughed, too.

"Bia, you are glorious." He leaned to regard her. "And there is not a mark on you, unlike me."

Adrian began to lick her skin like a cat, nibbled and bit her. Bia writhed with the intensity of it. He nursed her nipples until she thought she would go mad, so she pulled his hair and bit his ear. They rolled over the bed.

"You minx!" he howled, as she bit his arm.

"Ho, that will teach you."

"No, woman, I am going to teach you. Prepare yourself to be mine."

His blue eyes glittered and danced, and Bia was suddenly afraid. She would get up. Had they not done enough for now? Surely, she could…but he shifted his weight and towered over her. He was gigantic, what should she do?

A thorough kiss, his tongue seeking out hers to nip and taunt. Adrian's large hands gripped her; he was heavy. Her lungs would collapse; she would not survive. He gently parted her legs. Bia went on high alert, every sense strained.

"Say you love me, Bia," he said.

"Mmmm, yes, I love you madly, Adrian. But ought we, that is—"

"Sssshhhh. Do not speak except to say you want me inside you."

A flush of awareness passed over her skin. Bia wanted everything he would bring. "I do, Adrian.

Please, show me."

He smiled, his hair golden, his body satisfying and manly, his musky scent pleasant. "This first time," he warned, "may involve a brief pain, only once."

"I know," she mumbled. "Do not stop."

He balanced on his arms, how heroic of him. Put himself, his member now rigid, long, and firm, against her, there. Hot and heavy, demanding entrance. Her throat dry, she swallowed and tried not to hold back.

Adrian did not stop kissing and caressing her until Bia felt warm and safe, then he pressed forward, increased his weight and her senses twirled. He pushed in, but only a little, and she waited, then a thrust and a sharp sting. Bia started, trembled to her feet, and he was inside her body. She was astonished at the feel of it, enormous, hard, soft.

He moaned and held her tightly. "Bia, Bia, I never want to hurt you."

"It was nothing," she whispered. "Just love me."

Adrian thrust deeper still, lifting her to him. It was glorious, superb, unexpected, yet strangely familiar. He was powerful in his strength, his experience, knowledge, and expertise. He withdrew, and the mood shattered like glass. Then, back he came, stronger than ever, his whole body heated.

Desire swept through her, her heart pounded, she began to perspire. A rhythm in his strokes began, and Bia answered his every move. The emotional pitch, the giddy elation, the sounds they made, flesh to flesh. The human intimacy, seized by them from the ages, from all loving that had gone before.

The force of him increased as she rose to meet his thrusts. She tingled, shivered, and trembled keeping up with Adrian. Holding on, beleaguered, befuddled. Lost in a maelstrom, sinking down into a chasm. Then she was taken up and up. Soared free, strained, and sweated, as every particle of her flesh shook violently. Ribbons of flame snaked over her skin, and she sank into ecstasy.

Adrian halted his movements. His muscles standing out, he gazed into her eyes, and she saw his soul. "Bia, my only love," he murmured, shuddered, and she felt his release, a spurt of heat deep inside her. His seed, she gloried, his life, and now it was all hers. Bia held him tightly, kissed and caressed wherever she could reach, and loved Adrian entirely.

Adrian eased his weight from Bia but kept her in his arms. Their combined body heat quickly dried their skin. His chest heaved as he regained his breath. "Oh, my sweet, was it all right?"

She ran her fingers over his cheek and along his jaw. "Not exactly. More like a glimpse of paradise. Or like being loved by the whole planet. You carry such high emotion and are a most skillful lover. It seemed…the realization of a dream I cannot remember having. A secret dream of passion."

It was beyond thrilling. "I never experienced that kind of elation before. I never loved anyone, Bia. As a younger man, I took anything offered, but knew it was only a hint of what it could be if I cared. As I care for you." He shifted on the pillows, his shoulder and arm burning and painful from the exercise.

"So lovely to say, Adrian." She studied him. "Your shoulder hurts? Oh, my dear."

"No matter. It was worth it."

"How can I comfort you?"

"Kisses, lots of kisses, while I look at you."

Bia knelt over him, and he remembered the times at the cottage when she had cared for him. Tonight, she had come to him as his wife. To lovingly heal him from all his other injuries. She caressed his face, chest, and belly, her glossy hair in a lazy fall. Kissed him and whispered his name.

What a woman, he marveled, loving and smart, and ahead of him in all things if he was not careful. So lovely and graceful, her long hair tousled, her nakedness wholly natural. He was covered in abject adoration and did not give a fig who knew. Bianca would make him a better man, as his wife. Adrian could not wait for the transformation.

****

Bia lay with Adrian as he dozed. The whole room was scented with their presence, and the lovemaking had been celestial. She pulled the comforter over them.

What a long way they had come in a short time. From the first, incidents had all fallen into place as if following a plan. Adrian was her husband, the future stretching out before them. There would be troubles, sorrow, and joy, but they would take it as it came.

She would remember every detail for always. Her love for Adrian was all encompassing. Letty would find her way, and everything was so magical, Woof might even remember how to bark, and they would all be happy. She cuddled next to Adrian, and half asleep, he took her into his arm. All was well. The castle was surrounded by friends.

Bia thanked the gods for her blessings and would strive to deserve them. In the potential of it all, she went to sleep, to dream of tomorrow, safe in the loving embrace of now.

A word from the author...

I have a BFA in Studio Art and spent my career as a painter and sculptor. I came to New Mexico from the East Coast and began writing contemporary romance / mystery novels, set in a small ranching community near Santa Fe.

Soon Regency period historicals captured my main interest. I strive to portray intelligent, self-aware characters and maintain a solid story line, and I include a cheerful amount of sex.

https://www.jeanettecollinshighdesertart.com